PERENNIAL GIRL

J.E. Stamper

I greatly appreciate you taking the time to read my book.
Please consider leaving a review wherever you bought the book
and telling your friends about it.

Thank you so much for your support.

For Sophie, my special girl.

You make my life beautiful.

Before you read <u>Perennial Girl</u>, check out the free prequel story!

Visit the link below to receive a free eBook and audiobook version!

https://www.jestamper.com/sign-up

Chapter 1

IT'S HOT FOR a late-September midnight. Too hot. A busted old fan grinds out a pitiful stream of lukewarm air across my sweaty face. It'd be much cooler if I'd open a window, but there's this long-haired, freaky-looking guy sitting on the sidewalk outside. He's dressed in a holey, once-white tank top, and he keeps glancing back toward my window. I don't think he can see me lying here sweating on the threadbare sofa, but I swear it feels like he's looking right at me.

I'd go get in bed with Mom because she has one of those nifty window air conditioners in her room, but her door's locked tight. I'd have to burn the house down to even have a chance of waking her up, so I don't even bother knocking. Besides, who knows who's in there with her? I might hope to wake Mom only to find a grumpy, half-asleep stranger with a loaded gun at the door. Sounds dramatic, but it's happened before.

I'm sweaty and miserable, but I'm not hot enough or stupid enough to take that chance.

So here I am, simmering, waiting out another night while other kids in comfy beds tucked in tight with love dream the dark away. Somewhere along the way, my dreams got swallowed up by the Ugly. Once upon a time, there was a version of me who fell back into soft, safe sleep every night, dreaming dreams I mostly can't remember now. But I know they were sweet and gentle.

But now, as I melt into the smelly fibers of our scavenged throwaway sofa, my eyelids are projector screens showing slideshows of horror stories. In them, a bloody girl stumbles from hurt to hurt, dodging monsters who kill with razor-sharp words and poisonous looks.

In a lot of horror flicks, you know the hero is probably going to be okay. Sure, they'll get the crap kicked out of them a few times, but in the end, the police finally arrive and pull the mask off the monster and haul him to jail.

But here's the messed-up thing about my story, about the things that chase me behind my closed eyes: the monsters are real. They wear masks that look like my mom, like Headband Girl and her friends from my science class, like my math teacher, like the hundreds of other faces who spit out hatewords or look at me like they want to hurl, like the man with the weird head and rotten teeth who tried to do God-knows-what to me, like my dad.

I wait for someone to swoop in and unmask these creatures, to bind up their claws and yank out their teeth, to take them away and whisk me into a happily ever after.

I've been waiting a long time.

But I don't know how much longer I can wait before they gobble me up, *chomp chomp chomp.*

I give up trying to sleep for right now. I sit up and grab my backpack. I root around, hoping to find some leftover leftovers from the cafeteria today, some forgotten edible treasure buried within the depths of my bag. My fingers feel the crinkle of thin plastic. Jackpot. I pull out a little bag of carrot sticks. I'm not sure how long they've been in there, but they don't look too old. A little shriveled, maybe, but they don't smell so bad.

I sit and munch in the semidark of the front room. The street lamps bleed in a little shadowy light, but I'm afraid to turn on the lights inside. We don't have curtains, so if I light it up in here, I'm on full display to the weirdo outside. Meanwhile, I'd be blind as a freaking bat to him and the rest of the night dangers out there.

The carrots only seem to make me hungrier. My stomach growls and claws at me, trying to threaten me into giving it more. I'd brought home some leftover applesauce and raisins from the school cafeteria, but they are poor substitutes for actual food of the belly-filling variety.

When I got home today, I opened the door to find a takeout pizza box on the kitchen counter. My little heart leapt a bit, and my hopes of having an actual meal at home with Mom rose to new heights. But when I opened the box, those hopes came crashing down in a fiery wreck. Burning shrapnel everywhere. The thing was empty except for a few grease stains and a couple of cast-off black olive slices. I tasted an olive slice, but I spit it back out. Who the hell likes those things, anyway?

They remind me too much of myself. Spit out, cast away, discarded. Unwanted.

I pull out my math homework. Ms. Odum gives us a zillion math problems every night. Most of the time, I don't even bother with them. By the time I've made it home in the afternoon, I've got more pressing matters to attend to. Figuring out how many apples Kimmy has left over after selling 35 percent of them or calculating the circumference of a bunch of circles has a way of losing urgency when I've got to figure out how to survive another night in this hellhole.

But little does my witch of a math teacher know, my life is full of math problems.

Randi and her mom are talking to some lady from social services again. How many lies will they have to tell so that Randi's mom won't get hauled away? Bonus Question: How hard will Randi get her butt kicked as soon as the lady is out of sight, even though she's not the one who called social services?

If the little space beneath the fridge is two inches tall, eight inches deep, and 30 inches wide, how many packs of ramen noodles can Randi hide in it so that her mom won't find them and eat them while she's at school?

If Train A leaves the station traveling south at 50 miles per hour, how long will Randi have to wait on the tracks before it comes along and puts her out of her misery?

I'm pretty good at my kind of math, but Ms. Odum's meaningless numbers all blur together under the half-light of the living room. The anorexic moon outside tells me that it's around midnight. I give it an honest-to-goodness try, knowing that it won't be good enough anyway. Hunger, sweat, and exhaustion interfere with my calculations, and I know that what I'm scribbling there in the darkness will look like a bunch of nonsense when daylight comes around. At some point, as I read through the third problem for the fifth or sixth time, my eyes close and stay that way.

At least until my sleeping ears hear something on the front porch.

Chapter 2

I JOLT AWAKE, still clutching my pencil in one hand. I hear a *snap* as the lead breaks against my notebook. I'm in that confused type of almost-awakeness that so often happens when the nightmares scare a sleeping me back into real life.

But this time is different. My danger senses are all going haywire. Alarm bells are ringing in my head, even though I have no clue why. I sit on the sofa, barely breathing, listening with every muscle in my body.

But listening for what?

My heart is pounding hard against my ribs, so my breath comes out in little machine gun gasps. I sit there, clutching my broken pencil like a pitiful little dagger, waiting. A scared little bunny rabbit. I feel blood throbbing in my sweaty temples.

Nothing. Only dark silence broken by the hammering in my chest. Every nightmare image runs rapid-fire through my mind. This time, my scared little girl brain adds layers, painting my normal terrors with darker shades of evil, adding fears of new and unfelt pains from unfamiliar monsters.

So much ugly to be had here in the dark.

Then I hear it, a crunching, scraping noise on the front porch. With it, rough and grainy whispershouts in strange voices.

"Shit, man! What did you do?" one voice says.

"Shh! Hell if I know. Damn step broke or something. Shut up and help me get my foot out," says another one.

"Gonna wake up the whole damn neighborhood, man," says the first again. There's a little commotion. Sounds of splintering wood and tearing fabric and muttered curses. Whoever it is must have hit that second step and broken through. I hope old wood and rusty nails bite him deep and hit an artery or something.

But I know I'm not that lucky.

I'm frozen in a block of ice here in this 90-degree room. I'm stuck, wanting to run, scream, do something. But my pounding heart nails me down to this old sofa while the sounds continue on the other side of rotting wood and thin, cheap glass.

There are heavy, hateful footsteps on the porch just outside the front door.

"You think they heard us?" a whispering questioner asks.

"Don't think so," says the other. A *scrape-flick*, a quick flash of light, the smell of a cigarette.

"You an idiot? Put that out, man!" These words are angry and cut through louder than the ones before.

"Shut up!" says Idiot.

"You sure this is her house?" asks Not-Idiot. Who is this *her*? Are they talking about me? I start to shake all over. Little terror tears form ranks in my eyes.

"Yeah. He said he saw him go in here with her this afternoon," says Idiot. Not me. Mom. They're here for Mom.

What has she gotten us into this time?

"Okay," says Not-Idiot, "let's do this, then."

Oh God, oh God, oh God! What is happening? What is happening?

The door explodes inward with a sound that shakes the world. Two big shapes fill the doorway, silhouetted against the sick streetlight yellow. One of them holds what looks like a baseball bat. Their shadows, tall, dark, and mean, take over my life and fill up my little corner of Earth.

One of them takes a step forward. I break the heavy silence with a little involuntary squeal. I hear a little *click*, and fierce light fries my eyes to little scared crisps.

"Dammit! He didn't say nothin' about no kid, man," says one.

"Hell I'm supposed to know there's a kid here?" says the other.

I hold my hand over my eyes, trying to shield them from the painful glare. I can't see a thing. I'm a sweaty little sitting duck.

"I ain't messing with no kid, man, we'll do him next chance we get." says the first. "I'm out." Angry footsteps beat the floorboards and trail out the doorway and into the street.

Other footsteps come closer. I'm still a trembling, stinking mess, blinded by fear and bright white light. Something cold and metal is pressed hard against my cheek, squishing my cheek against my teeth. I taste penny copper blood.

Harsh words whisper in my ear. I can feel his breath. It smells like cigarettes and hot meanness. "Not a word about this to anyone! You got that? You run your ugly trap about this to anyone, and I'll find out about it and make you regret it."

I say nothing. My breath, ragged and broken, has forgotten how to make words.

The metal bites deeper and presses my head against the sofa. "You got that?"

I manage a weak little nod.

"Good," he spits back at me.

I squeeze my eyes shut. My eyelids are sponges, squishing out warm tears. The metal thing leaves my face, and the heavy footsteps pound out the doorway and into the night.

The ice covering my bones finally melts, and I run up to the door and slam it closed. Instead of latching like a normal, self-respecting door, it bounces back and almost pounds me in the face. I flick on the light (because stealth mode went to crap the second those creeps kicked in my door) and look at the damage. The dirty floor is covered in shards and splinters, and the wood all around the little lock thingy that sticks into the door frame is all busted up. There's no way that thing will lock now.

I look around for something to bar the door with, and suddenly my house looks so broken and empty. I mean, I know this place has always been a craphole, but now it feels like the crappiest craphole in this whole crapholey corner of the world. Before, at least, I could hope to lock the crazies out of my own little craphole.

When I was little kid, I watched this video in science class about bugs who shed their hard exoskeletons to create new, bigger ones for growing bodies. But after they crawl out of their

7

armor, it takes a while for the new suit to harden. And until that happens, birds and bigger bugs can scoop them up and gobble their soft little bodies. They've got to be good at hide-and-seek, at blending in when they're all squishy. Otherwise, they're dead meat for whatever hungry thing comes along.

That's how I feel. I'm this squishy, vulnerable little thing. After I finally wizened up after my life went to crap, I played at having this tough exterior, this "I don't take any crap from anyone, so don't even try it" front. I thought the world would just leave me alone if I looked bad enough and acted the part a little bit. I never really wanted to be a bad kid, but pretending to be one kept the tearing claws and sharp teeth at bay.

For the most part, anyway.

I wore that costume for a long time, but lately it's been rotting and falling off piece by piece. I try to keep my armor oiled and polished to convince everyone to leave me alone, but the tears that come a million times a day make it all rusty and weak. Then the hurts just break through and shatter little pieces of me away.

And now, now I'm a slimy, skeletonless bug just waiting to be devoured. I dart around the ruined house, one eye searching for something to give me at least a tiny sense of security, the other glued to the windows, waiting on a new predator to come along and gobble me up. I grab a busted old chair from the kitchen, this rusty metal thing with a bare seat, and shove it under the doorknob and jam the door closed. It seems to work like a charm in the movies, but I don't have much faith in it.

I grab the ratty, stinking cushions off the sofa and drag them to the bathroom. I stuff them into the bathtub and climb on top. I reach over and lock the door. It's got one of those clicky knob locks, but it's super easy to kick the flimsy door in. I know this because--well--I just do.

I spend the rest of the night sort-of sleeping in the bathtub, clutching my little pencil dagger, waiting.

Chapter 3

FEEBLE RAYS OF morning shining through the little bathroom window lull me to real sleep at some point.

I snap awake, and prescription-strength sunlight tells me that I've totally overslept. I don't know what time it is because I don't have a phone and my mom is still dead to the world, but I know school must have started at least a couple of hours ago.

I think about just skipping school for a minute. It might be nice to get away from all the crazy middle school bullcrap for a day. Just thinking about taking a break from some of the jerks at school spreads a buttery little smile across my face, even after last night's ordeal. But a gnawing emptiness in my stomach kicks my scrawny butt into gear.

I feel so lost and alone at school, but there's absolutely nothing for me here. And I mean *nothing*. No food, no prospects, nothing between me and the monsters except a rotten, now-broken door.

I think about last night. Those guys were looking for a *him*. Not for Mom, but for whoever's in there with her. I'm not sure what she's gotten mixed up in, but I've got to warn her. I go peck on her door, but no one answers. I don't knock too hard because I'm sure Mom'd be super pissed at me if I woke her up.

I scribble a little note and stuff it under her door. *"Guys came looking for your boy. Bad news. One of them had a gun I think. Be careful. See you after school."*

I unwedge the chair from the front door and swim out into a too-humid morning. The air presses moist and hot against my skin, and I think long and hard about just turning around and slamming the door on this whole day. But then again, who knows when Mom will finally get up or what kind of mood she's going to be in when she finally comes to. And I don't even want to think about being in the house if what's-his-name gets up first.

My stomach ends the debate for good, though.

Feed me.

I've got to go to school. I may have to stumble and hide my way through this crappy day, but at least I'll eat.

My taped-up shoe scrubs along the pavement. It holds better than I would've thought, but I have to change the tape every few days, and the roll of tape that Vulture Lady gave me is getting pretty thin. A few kids gave me crap about it for a while, but I told a kid in the cafeteria that the next person who said a word about my shoe would need to have it surgically removed from their butt.

Or something like that, but with a light sprinkling of a few choice words, and with the volume cranked up to a room-silencing, "This Girl Has Issues" level. I spent two days in detention for that little outburst, but it was worth it. No one said anything about my shoe after that. In fact, most people steer clear these days.

I like it like that. The fewer people who pretend that I exist, the fewer people who engage me in human contact, the less likely I am to go completely berserk and unleash the Ugly.

She's so close these days, this Ugly Me. After last night, I don't know how long I can hold her off.

I slog on like some zitty, adolescent zombie, shuffling my tired feet down this filthy street. A little trickle of traffic zooms by, but no one bothers to take notice of my truant little self. Besides the occasional car and the un-Septemberlike sticky heat, though, it's one of those storybook mornings. The sun filters cheery and bright down through clouds that look like they've been painted onto blue canvas. A gazillion birds join their morning songs into this constant twitter-chirp orchestra. It's really something.

But what am I among all this pretty stuff? My dirty clothes, my worn-out, falling-apart shoes, my smelly, too-skinny body? Where do I fit in in this picture? I'm pretty sure I'm just a smudge, a little splatter of paint, a failed brush stroke.

A mistake.

I picture that cheerful T.V. painter guy with the fro. If he saw me walking along next to his happy little trees under the shade of his happy little clouds, he'd probably scrape me off with his paint knife thing or smudge me into a happy little grease stain on the sidewalk.

My elementary school art teacher always told us that mistakes just make the art better, more real. But this big mistake of *me*, always tumbling along like garbage in the wind? What could I possibly contribute? Tears sting my eyes and drip down. One of them lands on the duct tape holding my shoe together and sits there like a tiny little puddle. In it, I see the sky reflected bright blue.

I wish I could shrink myself down into that minuscule globe. I could be in there all alone under that sky. No noise, none of this nonsense, this constant ugly, the hate, the anger, the hurt. Just me, all alone and quiet and content inside my bright little bubble.

I stand there for a few minutes imagining what life could be like without the noise and the mean. What would I think about then? What would I do? Will I ever get to a place away from all this bullcrap? Away from the name-calling, away from the hurtful looks, away from the pain?

I used to think maybe so, but after last night, I'm not so sure.

I sniff loud and ugly and wipe snot all down the sleeve of my ratty aqua-blue hoodie. I saw it in the lost and found a couple of weeks ago. It didn't look like total trash and didn't totally smell like butt, but it was smeared with just enough filth and age that I figured I'd be able to sneak it home without Mom noticing that I had something new. She gets super childlike jealous of those kinds of things sometimes. I checked on it every day for, like, a week to make sure it was still there. Once I figured that its absentminded former owner had forgotten it for good, I snagged it and took it home.

I've worn it 24/7 since then, even though it's been too hot for a hoodie. I don't know. Sometimes, when I feel like I'm going to explode, I throw up the hood and kind of turtle down into it and shut the world out. It pisses off the authorities when I do that, but it's better than the alternative.

I'd much rather be weird, stubborn Turtle Girl than crazy, dangerous Ugly Me.

I keep walking and eventually pass by God's Grace Church. It's this building that looks like someone stapled a steeple on an airplane hangar. It's surrounded by this chainlink fence with prison-style barbed wire at the top. Just inside the fence is one of those signs with the moveable letters. It says "All Welcome." You don't have to be a genius to see the irony in that one.

I went there one time not too long ago. I found a flyer for this event that promised fun and food and stuff like that. I used Mom's phone to call the number, and this rickety old church van/bus thing showed up at my house. When I got in, the driver, this middle-aged guy with a comically-wide tie, wrinkled his nose and gave one of those disgusted looks. He didn't say anything on the way there, but when he brought me back home, he sure had something to say.

"Hey kid," he said as I turned to close the door.

"Yeah," I said, expecting a churchy something in return. Maybe a bit of advice or a little nugget of encouragement to take the edge off my crappy existence. Some kind of nice, foreign-sounding Jesus-y thing to keep me warm until next time. Something with a chapter and a verse.

"I'm not trying to be mean, but maybe you should think about taking a bath or something before next time. Some of the other people complained." I felt like I'd been punched in the gut. I just stood there, mouth open like a trout, too stunned for any kind of bitchy little comeback. He gave me this uncomfortable-looking smile and leaned over and shut the door in my face.

Salty tears stung my eyes, and I stared hurt and hate at the van's dingy taillights as it puttered away.

What would Jesus do?

I don't know a lot about church stuff, but I'm guessing he'd want to kick that guy's butt.

I continue eyes-down in my sweaty, sleep-deprived trudge until a sudden blast of sound from behind gives me a miniature heart attack. I turn, ready to bolt...

Chapter 4

I SPIN AROUND, claws out, ready to shred someone's face off or jet down an alleyway or blast off to the moon or something. And if I'm not mistaken, I think a little pee came out in the process. Great. Just what I needed.

But when my frantic brain is finally able to focus, what I see is not some killer psycho or a rabid animal.

It's a police car.

And I'm somehow standing in the middle of the street like a total doofus. I guess I wandered out here while I was daydreaming (daynightmaring?). I guess I'm lucky I wasn't creamed by some a-hole checking his email behind the wheel.

Or, I don't know. Maybe I'd be better off as a bloody, broken hood ornament.

The officer must've done that chirpy, almost-cute *whoop-whoop* thing with the siren when he pulled up to me. He opens the door and puts a black-booted foot down heavy on the pavement. I think about bolting, but that probably wouldn't end too well for me. He looks pretty fit, and I don't think this half-starved, sleep-deprived little me would stand a chance. He stands up tall and straight and puts on a very policey frown.

He takes a couple of steps toward me. All the leather pouches and other stuff on his belt creak and jangle in the stuffy air. Guns and ammo and handcuffs and pepper spray and tasers and all kinds of mean, hurting things. He takes another step, and I tense even more.

When I was little, I had this wind-up blue bunny rabbit that

Mom and Dad gave me in my Easter basket. I remember seeing it there, half-buried in that plastic fake grass stuff surrounded by a million little jelly beans. I loved that thing. I'd wind it up *crank, crank* for what seemed like forever until the little spring inside felt so tight that I thought the whole thing would burst. Then I'd let it go and watch it skitter and whizz all over the place while Dad ate the gross black jelly beans that made me gag but he swore were the best kind once you got a taste for them.

I'd laugh and they'd laugh because I was laughing, knowing that they'd created this precious little Hallmark Channel moment.

How long has it been since I've laughed at home? I can't even remember.

I'm the wind-up bunny now--cranked up so tight that I'm either going to explode into a hundred sharp plastic shards or just go crazy and scuttle around like mad until I'm worn down to a useless little lump.

Officer Police Guy must have noticed me tense up because he stops in his tracks and holds his hands out, palms open toward me in a "Okay, now take a chill pill because I promise I'm not going to hurt you" way. Neither of us says anything for a few seconds.

"You okay, kid?" he finally asks. "You were just kind of standing there in the middle of the street. Didn't even hear me drive up. I don't want you to get hit or anything."

I manage a weak little nod. Am I okay, though?

"Okay. Where you headed? Shouldn't you be in school right now?" he says, relaxing his hands a little bit but still keeping them away from all the scary stuff on his belt. Sunlight glints off the nameplate on his chest. *Anderson.*

My mouth is, like, total Sahara right now, but I squeeze out a few words. "Um, yeah. I overslept. Uh, headed there now." I motion toward the general direction of the school. Some of the tension melts from his face. Not a truant street rat; just an irresponsible bozo. "My mom had to go to work early, and I fell back asleep. Then when I woke up, I kind of freaked out and ran right out the door." The lies spill out free and easy and collect into a puddle at my feet. So much easier to lie than to speak the truth. But one of these days, I know I'm going to drown.

"Well, let me give you a ride, then. Don't want to see you get squashed. Besides, you look like you're about to melt," he says with a little smile. He nods over to his cruiser. I stand still, a frozen girl on this hot pavement.

Nope. Not today. No way I'm getting into that thing. Been there, done that. It didn't end well. I'm ready to make like a bunny rabbit and take my chances.

He notices. He says nothing. He walks around the car and opens the front passenger door. "Come on. I'll let you ride up front," he says.

He puts on a smile. "It's alright," he says, "I just want to make sure you get there in one piece."

I hesitate for a little bit longer. I just started my day, but I'm already exhausted and achy. I haven't had a real meal since yesterday's lunch. It wouldn't hurt to save a few steps. My legs thaw and carry me to the car.

He holds the door open for me. I kind of have to finagle myself into the seat because there's so much stuff scattered around. It's like some sort of garbage bomb went off in here or something. There are a few greasy food wrappers and empty coffee cups in the floor, and some serious-looking police equipment stuff is scattered around like debris after a storm. I look over at the driver's seat. It's pitiful. The yellow foam is poking through the cloth all over the place. It looks worse than the ratty, threadbare sofa in my house. The whole place has this lived-in feel to it, and it kind of makes me sad in a weird type of way.

I try to guess how much time he spends in here all alone, watching, listening to the radio chatter, thinking. Waiting for garbage like me to do something stupid. Wondering if the next call that his radio spits out will be the last he hears.

I steal a glance through the holes in the metal cage between the front and back. The seats are hard plastic, spotless, scrubbed clean with some kind of smelly disinfectant. The smell sort of makes me queasy.

Just being me makes me queasy.

The last time I saw Dad was from the outside of a police car. Harsh blue lights flashed in my eyes, blinding me in short little bursts. But through the flashes I could still see him looking back at me with eyes I didn't recognize.

Kind blue eyes which used to look with so much love and tenderness replaced by red wet things staring anger and hate. The eyes I used to wait for every afternoon were gone.

I still see them in old photos sometimes. When I can bear to look at them, that is. When I can cut through the blue lights in my memory and remember what those eyes meant to me in the before times.

I feel my eyes now, leaking pain onto my cheeks. I shake the thoughts and the tears away. How long have I been standing here at this open door?

What is wrong with me?

Chapter 5

I SETTLE MYSELF in among the debris. He closes the door. Not a vicious *slam*, but a gentle *click*. I feel like an invader, like I've just crash-landed on an alien planet or something like that. The harsh hospital smell of the disinfectant mingled with the scent of sweat suffocates me. My breath comes faster and faster until I'm seriously worried that I'm going to pass out. The sides of the car start to close in and threaten to smash me into a greasy pulp.

What am I doing here? How did I get here? My scrawny, dirty hand scrabbles around for the door handle.

A sudden voice from my left makes me jump and startles me back to life. A scared little bunny rabbit squeal rushes out of me.

"Hey, hey. It's okay," says the voice. He's sitting in the car next to me. I didn't even hear him sit down or close the door.

Where is my mind today?

His voice has lost its police-ness and has softened into a warm blanket. He no longer sounds like some testosterone-fueled authority figure tweaked out on adrenaline. I look over in the direction of his words. He wears a slight frown under a pair of concerned eyes. Not blue, thank God, but a deep brown the color of chocolate cake.

"Really, are you okay?" he asks.

"I...uh...yeah," I say. "I guess I'm just a little lightheaded from the walk." Am I lying this time? I can't even remember.

"Here, then," he says. He digs around and pulls out something wrapped in crinkly plastic. It's one of those chocolate and peanut butter Nutty Pal cake things. He hands it over to me. "Take this. God knows you need it more than I do." He laughs and pats his belly. He's not really pudgy at all, but I know what he's trying to do.

But I'm too hungry and too tired to do that thing where you have to pretend you don't want something the first time it's offered to you just to be polite. Before I can stop myself, I grab the thing out of his hands. Well, "snatch" is probably closer to the truth. I rip it open with dirty, hungry claws without even looking at him and begin stuffing it into my pie hole.

I don't know if it's just because I'm a hungry mess, but it's, like, the best thing I've ever tasted. The sugary overload gives me a case of the instant warm-and-fuzzies, and before I know it, I've eaten half of the thing without even taking a breath. When my brain finally catches up and realizes what an ugly wild animal I'm being, I feel my cheeks burn. I drop my hands into my lap.

"Sorry," I say in a quiet, embarrassed voice. "Thank you. I really appreciate it."

"Don't mention it," he says. "You're very welcome."

He puts the car into gear and drives slowly. I munch on the rest of the Nutty Pal, trying to be a little bit less of a complete and total pig this time. We ride along in silence for a bit. While I'm chewing, he opens his mouth a couple of times to say something, but no words escape. His face wears a concerned expression.

He tries again.

"So when's the last time you ate something?" he finally manages to spit out.

So there it is. I silently curse myself for being here right now and for acting like a total starved loser. I might as well have just turned on a big, flashy neon sign.

Pity Me! Pity Me! Pity Me!

So what am I supposed to do? Lie again? I try to think about the lies that I've already told today. It's so hard to remember the truth when I have to constantly tread water in my lies. It's exhausting. I've heard people say that thing about truth setting you free. And every time my scrawny butt lands in the school office, Mr. Gorley always tells me that the best thing to do in any situation is to just tell the truth.

Any person who says that obviously doesn't know crap about my life. In my lousy existence, the truth buys fresh bruises and shiny new heartaches.

"My mom made me breakfast just before I left," I say. I go back to nibbling, and the car rumbles on.

He doesn't say anything else for a second, but then the car lurches as he swings it over to a stop next to the curb. I rattle around in my seat like a little sack of bones.

He turns and gives me a look that pins me against the seat. "You said that your mom went to work and you fell asleep and made a mad dash out the door when you woke up," he says. His voice doesn't carry any anger, but it has lost its candy coating.

My head dips under the surface, and my lungs fill with cold water. *Splash.* I cough and sputter and try to think of yet another whopper.

He sees me trying to talk and holds up his hand. "Listen, kid," he says in that serious business tone. "I'm not an idiot. I don't expect you to tell me everything. I mean, we just met. You're smart not to tell me everything." He sighs and gives a little chuckle. "I know you've got no reason to trust me, but listen. I--"

His voice cracks, and he breaks off and turns to face the driver's side window. His leg starts to shake a little, bouncing up and down and making little *zoot, zoot* noises as it swishes against the threadbare seat. He takes a deep, shuddery breath and speaks again.

"I have a daughter about your age. Actually goes to your school," he says and gestures up the street. "The thing is...well...I was a major screw-up when she was little. Too young to have a kid, you know? Did a lot of stupid things, me and her mom both. And one of those stupid things--"

He breaks off again and turns away from me. His leg shakes harder against the seat. I can feel the car bounce along with it. He wipes at his eyes.

What is happening?

"One of those stupid things got her mom killed. After that, I just gave up for a while. Lost custody of her to her mom's folks," he says to the window. He scrubs his eyes again.

"I--I'm sorry," I say, not knowing if I'm supposed to say anything, really. *Why is he telling me this?* I look down at my lap.

He waves my words away. "They take really good care of her. Better than I ever could." He sniffs and turns to me. I look up, and he locks onto me with red-brown eyes shiny with wet.

"Do you ever get to see her?" I ask.

"Yeah," he says. "I've really been trying these last couple of years. Cleaned myself up. Got a good job." He gestures down at his uniform. "I get to see her sometimes now." He looks out the window again and sighs.

A few cars creep by and hit their brakes. I see their occupants rubber-necking. We must be quite the spectacle.

"But it's hard, you know. Visiting her, knowing that when it's over, she's not coming home with me," he says. He gives a sad, slobbery chuckle. "Anyway--Jesus--you don't need to know all this. My point is, looking at you this morning standing in the street all alone made me think of my daughter. Made me think of all my screw-ups and what that's done to her. Her grandparents are nice and take real good care of her, but it's gotta hurt, you know."

Yeah. I do know. Man, do I know. I don't say anything, but I give a little nod. My eyes begin that familiar burn.

"Look at me, kid," he says. For some reason, I obey and meet his watery eyes. "I don't know you, and I don't know your story. But I know what I'm looking at, and I know you deserve better."

I can't bear to look at him any longer, and I stare back down at my bony, dirty lap. Little spots of wet begin to appear on my jeans.

"Just...just hang in there, okay, kid?" he says. "Just hang in there. There's a reason for you, and one of these days, you'll find it."

I manage a weak little nod. "Okay," I whisper.

"Listen, the officer at your school is my buddy. We used to run a lot of calls together. He's a good guy. You know him?"

I sniff, snotty and loud. "Yeah," I say.

"I'm going to get him to look out for you, okay?"

"Okay," I say. Ugly Me pops up out of nowhere and sounds the alarm. *What are you agreeing to? Do you really want someone like that sniffing around?*

"What's your name, kid?" he asks.

Ugly Me comes on loud and mean. *Lie! Lie! Lie!*

I hesitate. *What do I do?* Warning bells chime, and my heart begins to pound in my chest. This kind of attention could bring a lot of bad stuff down on me. People like me don't survive long in the spotlight.

I take a deep breath.

"Miranda Lewis," I say.

Chapter 6

IN ORDER TO put the car back in drive, he has to do some kind of super-secret police voodoo with some hidden switches and stuff. It's like a little two-second police dance routine. I shoot him a raised eyebrow. He laughs.

"Anti-theft," he says. "When we're on calls, we sometimes leave the cars running even though we're not supposed to. The secret stuff keeps people from just hopping in and driving away."

I guess I didn't notice him do it the first time because I was too busy pigging out. "That's actually pretty cool. It's like some James Bond stuff," I say. It's nice to have a semi-normal conversation sans tears and deep, uncomfortable stuff. Ugly Me slinks into the background for a second, but my nerves are still on edge from the doozy of a conversation I just had with this guy who's basically a complete stranger.

It's been a weird day, and it's not even lunchtime.

He slides into traffic, and we chat it up about about some random stuff. Just a light sprinkling of conversation that doesn't really mean anything. Kind of a silence-filler, really. And after the talk we just had, that's just fine with me. I think a long, awkward silence right now might just kill us both.

It doesn't take long to get to the school. As I step out of the car, he says, "Good luck, kid. You've got this."

"Thanks," I say. "Thanks for everything. Really."

He nods his head and gives me a little salute. "Don't mention it."

I turn and face the school. It's super weird to show up this late, and I get that alien invader feeling again. But to be fair, I'm used to feeling like I don't quite belong here. Or anywhere else, for that matter. I'm some pitiful stray cat that people don't really want but keep around just to be nice. I look up and see a few faces looking back at me. I feel my face turn all tomato-y. For the millionth time today, I'm really tempted to turn tail and take my chances elsewhere. I wonder what people must think. I mean, it's not every day that a police car makes deliveries.

I try not to care what people think of me. I'm used to throwing up this nice, thick wall of don't-give-a-damn, but it's exhausting to maintain it with the looks and words always chipping away at it.

I take a few steps toward the school even though my legs feel like they weigh a zillion pounds. I look back, and Officer Anderson is still there. I guess he wants to make sure I actually go inside.

Smart guy.

I reach for the button on the doorbell camera thing, but my finger pauses. I think about last night. *Should I tell him?* Sure, I'm exhausted, but my tired legs could easily carry me back to the police car, back to someone who might actually be able to help me. Ugly Me slinks out of the shadows. My heart beats fast, and I close my eyes and press my hand to my cheek.

A dull pain reminds me and snaps me out of this stupid little fairy tale. If I tell and Officer Prince Charming starts sniffing around my house, then my ugly face is likely to end up staring out from that sad lost kids bulletin board at the supermarket.

Because after last night, the threat, the pain, the fear is so much more real to me than this little Officer Friendly charade.

But still, there was something there. Something in those fighting-back-tears eyes almost makes me want to trust.

Almost.

I reach over and press the button. The electrified microphone voice of Ms. Joan, the new school secretary, blasts harsh and loud out of the speaker. "Thought you'd never push that button, Hon. Come on in."

The door unlocks with a *ka-chunk*, and I pull it open. I step inside and take another look back. Officer Anderson gives a little salute and drives away. The door shuts behind me, and I make my way to the main office where Ms. Joan greets me with a sticky-sweet "Hey there, Hon." She's actually one of the few people in this building that I can stand on a consistent basis. To be fair, she's never in the difficult position of ordering me around when I don't want to be ordered around, and she never has to try to make me do anything I don't want to do. But she's just so super nice all the time and doesn't treat me like I'm a walking inconvenience with zits.

"Hi, Ms. Joan," I say.

"Mornin', Girlie," she says. When I get to the big desk/counter thing, she squints through her itty-bitty glasses at me. "Well bless your little heart. You look like you've had a rough mornin'." She's got this really thick country drawl thing going on. She talks with molasses words that just kind of drip out all slow and sweet. I normally love to hear her voice and usually try to stick around the office as long as I can to bask in her warmth, but this time, I'm in a hurry to jet out of there before I have to lie to her.

"Yeah, rough morning," I say. I don't offer any explanation.

"Well, Hon, if you need anything, you just come on down and let ol' Ms. Joan know, okay?" she says. Thankfully, she doesn't ask for details. She hands me a tardy slip, and her big hoop earrings jangle against her chubby cheeks.

I know I'm supposed to go straight to class, but I'm just not feeling it yet. I might just have a nuclear meltdown if I have to plop my butt down in a seat and sit quietly like a good little girl. After everything that's happened since last night, my mind is an exhausted mess. Thoughts zoom around in there like ricocheting bullets in some stupid video game. They give me a headache, and I'm afraid that if I'm not careful, they'll break out of my skull and tear everything apart.

I detour to the sacred middle school sanctuary to hang out for a bit. I don't see anyone when I walk in. That's some good luck. There are usually at least one or two hormonal headcases hanging out in the bathroom at any given time. But this time, my only company is a dripping faucet and some leftover farts.

But I'm more comfortable in a dirty, smelly bathroom than I am in class.

I pick a stall that looks the least like a toxic waste dump and take a seat. I don't even bother to pull down my pants to make it look like I'm going. I put my elbows on my knees and press my face into my hands.

"I swear to God I'll kill you if you tell anyone," he says. His breath is hot and dirty against the side of my face. The metal something digs into my cheek. I yell for Mom to come help. Her door swings open, and someone steps out.

But it's not Mom. I can't tell who it is in the dark, but it's a big, strong-looking man. The metal thing leaves my face, and *bang, bang, bang* rings my ears. Through flashes of light, I see Dad running to save me. More loud noises and flashes of light.

He doesn't fall but comes strong and fast and makes the bad man disappear. I'm shaking on the dirty sofa, and he looks down at me with happy blue eyes. He smiles and says--

"Randi Lewis, report to the office!"

My head snaps up out of my hands, and I feel a pang in my neck. My dark house disappears, and I'm in this stinky bathroom again. I shake my head and try to figure out what just happened.

"Randi Lewis, report to the office at once!" comes the voice again.

Chapter 7

I TURN THE handle on the hot water side of the faucet. I let it run for a second to wash a half-dry giant loogie down the drain. Society seems to think that girls are all prim and proper like clean little princesses. That must be the biggest joke of all time.

I'm not sure how we pulled that one off.

Because behind closed doors, we're just as gross as anyone else. We fart and spit and drip and sweat and leak, but we're just not as blatant about it.

The hot water finally turns from arctic to simply frigid, and I stick my hands under it. I watch little rivers flow cold and clean over my dingy skin. My hands are finally healing, and new, pink skin crisscrosses through the old. These scars are the only thing new and shiny about me, but they only remind me of what happened.

Is there a way for me to crawl into a new skin and leave the old behind?

Emmaline's ring still clings to my finger. I never take it off now, and it's scratched and stained. But I still know that the stars are there, locked away under the scrapes and dirt. She offered to take it home and clean it up with this special little buffer thing she has, but I'm too afraid to part with it even for a day.

"Miranda Lewis, report to the office immediately!" breaks through the sound of running water. It rushes out of the little speaker on the wall all loud and angry. I can't be sure, but it sounds like the cranky voice of Ms. Odum, my math teacher.

Great. The one bright spot in this whole crappy ordeal was that

I missed my daily mathematics torture session. Being in her class is like sitting in a dragon's lair. Except the dragon is a cranky, loud-mouthed menopausal wreck with a super-wide mean streak. And it wears horrible old lady perfume.

When I'm in the lair, it feels like she's constantly watching me through those little glasses, all perched behind her desk just waiting for me to put a toe out of line so she can gobble me up and spit out my bones. And despite my best-ish efforts, the numbers and letters she gives us make no sense to me. They jumble up and dance around the page and taunt me.

I take a deep breath and splash some more water on my face. I'd best just get this over with. If not, she'll just get madder and madder and end up sniffing me out anyway. She probably just wants to yell at me for not having my homework again. As I walk to the office, I begin thinking up yet another excuse that the old bat won't believe.

Because telling her the truth about last night is waaaaay out of the question. Not that she'd believe me anyway.

I walk into the office just as she picks up the intercom to spit flames into it again. I swear there are black scorch marks on the thing. She's standing behind Ms. Joan, and when I walk into the room, Ms. Joan gives me a pitiful "I'm so sorry about this" kind of look. I'll bet Dragon Lady bullied the intercom away from her.

"Where have you *been*, young lady?" blasts my way like a freight train. I flinch at the sound of the harsh hatewords. She puts her hand on her bony hip and lasergazes my way.

I feel the familiar scratching in my gut. Ugly Me begs to be released. Ugly Me is tired and scared and hungry and is chomping her sharp teeth, waiting for a moment like this. I take a deep breath and say nothing.

Because saying nothing is much safer than opening my mouth and saying what I want to say.

"And don't even try to lie to me and say you've been in class, Missy," she adds. Spooky. She must be reading my mind. Lies come smooth and easy for me, even ones that could get shot down with a simple email or phone call. "Because I went looking for you in Practical Arts, where you were *supposed* to be."

"I was in the bathroom. I'm not feeling well this morning. That's why I was late," I say. I muster enough strength to not yell or curse or give a smart-ass answer. It makes me feel like a regular Hercules.

"*Mmm-hmm*," she says with a snide little head wobble. "Let me just tell you what I think of *that* excuse--"

"Carol," interrupts Ms. Joan as she turns to lock eyes with the dragon. She's lost her sugary sweetness. Her voice has a surprising edge--not razor-y, but sharper than I would have expected from her. "Ms. Lewis is *here* now. Didn't you need her for something?"

Ms. Joan has her back to me now, but judging by the look in Ms. Odum's eyes, the two women are having an epic standoff. It's total silent war in here right now, and it's kind of giving me chills. I don't know whether to just stand here like a statue or jet out the doorway and run for the hills. But sweet Ms. Joan holds fast under that hot lava stare and Ms. Odum breaks off with a little "Hmmph."

She turns back to me. "Yes. I need you right now. You missed your benchmarking assessment this morning, so you're going to take it now," she says. She's a little bit deflated now and seems a little less dangerous. Not friendly, by any means, but not actively hating the sight of my dirty little carcass.

Crap. I hate those things with a passion. They're these super-hard tests on the computer that we have to take every few weeks to reveal to the authorities how much we've learned. Or, in my case, how much I haven't learned.

According to the little speech that the teachers had to memorize in case any of us little ungrateful delinquents asks why we have to take these stupid things, the tests are just for data collection to give the teachers an idea of how things are going. But you can tell the teachers hate them as much as we do. On the days leading up to the tests, the teachers chew antacids like candy. When the results come pouring in, they carry tear-soaked tissues and hold little support group sessions in the hallways after school.

It's pretty sad. If I thought Ms. Odum gave a damn about me, I might actually try on this thing.

Ms. Odum points a crooked, bony finger into the hallway, and walk out the door.

I make a mental note to bring Ms. Joan a bouquet of those yellowy flowers that grow in the abandoned lot near my old house. I'll have to dodge the broken glass and God-knows-what-else to get them, but she deserves it.

I wish she could just pack me up in that giant purse of hers and carry me home.

Chapter 8

I FOLLOW DRAGON Lady down the hallway toward some distant mystery torture chamber. I feel like I'm walking across hot coals and keep waiting for her to explode and melt me into a little puddle of adolescent goo. But for some reason, she doesn't say anything to me.

Whatever voodoo Ms. Joan just worked in the office has really done a number on her.

She scoots along in this fast little angerwalk. I'm kind of impressed. I didn't think she could move this quickly. Her pants make this *skeet, skeet* noise as she powers on, and I keep expecting to see smoke coming from between her thighs. I have to burn some serious rubber just to keep up with her for a few seconds. The tape running across the bottom of my shoe catches on the floor, and I stumble.

I totally don't mean to, but I put on a whole show of trying to catch my balance--flailing arms and loud, flapping, trying-to-catch-my-balance stompy steps. I manage to not fall on my face, but all the noise catches Ms. Odum's attention. She looks back at me; her eyes flicker with flames.

She inhales to breathe fire, but she stops short. Her eyes drift down to my feet. I follow them. The tape holding my shoe together is torn, and my sole flaps freely. She gets this funny look on her face and turns around and starts walking again.

She slows down a little bit, and I'm able to keep up without slamming my face into the floor. We stop outside a room I've never been in. She digs a key out of her pocket and opens the door. The room is the love child of a neglected storage unit and a low-rent conference room. A fancy, gigantic table sits in the middle of the room surrounded by these big, cushy blue fake leather chairs. The rest of the room is crowded with all kinds of cast-off teacher crap. Boxes full of old paper are stacked into several dangerous-looking leaning towers, a couple of dented file cabinets lurk in the corner, and this old TV cart is shoved against a scuffed-up wall.

The whole place smells like dust and feet. I really hope they don't have conferences in here with actual important people because this place is, like, crazy ghetto. But on the other hand, if these chairs had a few more rips and stains, I'd feel right at home.

"Have a seat and get started," she says. She points a skeleton finger at a computer set up on the table. Her voice has a sort of flatness to it. No edges at all. "And come up to my room when you're done."

I turn to answer her and probably give some grumpy, smarty-pants remark that'll get me in a bunch of trouble, but she scoots out of the room and closes the door before I can say anything. It's so weird. I spend a ton of time during school most days trying to find some quiet-ish place to hide out in, but now that I actually have permission to be all by myself, the whole idea has lost its shine. I'm used to hanging out in busy bathrooms, but this place is so quiet that it's kind of creepy.

The little fan in the computer behind me whooshes on and makes me jump. I spin around, ready to rumble. I feel like a doofus. Why the hell am I so jumpy today?

Splintering wood, cold metal against my face. Sleepless.

I remember.

The computer screen is facing the doorway, which means that I'll have to sit with my back to the door. This will not do. No, sir. No way. I scoot the computer around the table so that I sit facing the door. It makes a God-awful screeching racket as I slide it along, but no one comes to figure out what the heck all the noise is about.

When I plop into the chair, it squooshes out a giant hiss of stale air that smells mildly of old man B.O. The chair is comfortable and sinks in with me. My stomach makes a horrific growling noise. My insides feel like they're clawing at me. I'm so hungry. The Nutty Pal was amazing, but it did little to fill the dark pit inside me.

I stare at the computer for a couple of minutes before I manage to muster up the gusto to even get past the login screen. Luckily, the test is already set up and ready to go, so all I have to do is hit the big green "Begin Assessment" button. I don't think I have the energy right now to jump through very many virtual hoops, much less make any grade that isn't complete and utter fail sauce.

The first question of the test is about some kid named Miguel who is an aspiring music artist. I'm given a bunch of numbers, and I'm supposed to figure out how much money he makes if his YouTube channel gets X hits per day and if he sells Y records per month or something like that. I have no freaking clue how to work it out, but good for Miguel, I guess.

I used to have dreams and aspirations and all that. It was mostly fairy tale stuff about me being some big, successful something. But now, my biggest hopes and dreams are about getting out of this craphole town to somewhere far away and just finding a way to not be totally miserable all the time. And I still think about the stars sometimes, warm white specks of bright across a blanket of night. I still imagine lying down in the soft grass, maybe under a big, fuzzy blanket, warm with happy and love and just staring at the stars until I drift off to sleep.

I know he's just some fictional nothing in a math problem, but I hate Miguel for being more than a broke, starved nothing like me. I rage-click a random answer, and musical Miguel disappears forever.

I actually try some of these problems, but every time I think my brain is going to math something for a second, my stomach yells and demands all the attention like some loud, hungry diva.

There's no math in me today--only hunger and exhaustion.

I click a few answers without even looking at the problems, then the soft chair and quiet room send me to la-la land.

Chapter 9

I TILT MY head back and look at the stars. They go on and on and on in the ink spread across the sky. Beneath me is a blanket of soft green. I feel its cool touch against my skin as I lie there.

I'm alone here, and the grass and sky stretch out into the forever all around me. A warm breeze plays through the scene, and I'm safe and happy and everything I want to be.

The stars flicker and twinkle as I stare into them. They give me gentle, friendly little winks, and I know they see me, and I know they care. I feel loved and wanted here under these little pinholes of light. And even though it's dark all around, I'm not afraid because those little lights hold me in their power.

I'm not afraid and I'm not hungry and I'm not tired.

I am happy here under these stars.

I inhale deep and breathe in the everything around me. It's all so fresh and sweet and somehow smells like nothing and everything good all at the same time. There's nothing here to choke me--no smoke, no garbage, nothing that isn't fresh and good and pure.

I am happy here under these stars.

My legs and body and arms feel light and strong, but I'm happy just to lie here doing nothing inside all this happy. I could run forever with this body, but I don't need to. I can just stay here because there's nowhere else I want to be.

I cuddle in deeper to the soft grass, and it sends little thrills through my skin as it holds me deeper. I close my eyes, and a smile stretches across my face. I don't think about the ugly or the hurt because those things don't exist here. They can't touch me under this sky. My eyes lose themselves tracing outlines in the lights above me, and only happy and warm thoughts exist in my mind.

I hold my hands in front of my face. The night is dark, but the stars are bright enough to tell me that my scars are gone. I've got a new skin, new memories, new life.

My heart smiles for the first time in forever.

A bell dings hard and loud, and the stars scatter. They flee as harsh, fluorescent light floods my world. The grass is gone, too, and with it, my comfort.

And my happiness.

I'm back in my crappy reality with a sore neck and an empty stomach. I lift my head toward the computer screen. A pop-up with a little cartoon detective with a magnifying glass taunts me.

"Are You Still There?" it asks in big, bold bubbly letters. It threatens to shut the test down and alert the teacher if I don't respond. I click "Continue Test."

Am I still here? Why? Just a month ago I swore to myself that things would be different, that this year would be the one that would drag me out of my black hole. I swore that I'd kill Ugly Me once and for all and be a normal, non-crazy, non-miserable kid.

And despite my best efforts, despite being a good girl and not ripping anyone's lips off, despite showing up to school most days, despite making a couple of non-delinquent friends, I'm still here. I'm still a miserable, starved rat running around this maze, never finding the cheese--just finding dead end after dead end and breaking my nose against the walls.

How long can I keep this up? How long can Ugly Me stay hidden? She's always there now, simmering just below the surface, waiting to boil up and wreck lives.

My stomach gurgles again, deep and painful and empty. I panic for a second and look at the clock on the computer screen, praying that I haven't snoozed right through lunch. It's only 11:17. That's a huge relief. I've only been asleep for about 20 minutes. Maybe there is a God.

I don't even bother looking at the questions. *Click, click, click,* and I'm done in a cool five minutes. After I answer the last question, a little hourglass appears on the screen. It's calculating my score. Oh, goody. The suspense is just killing me. I can't wait to see how horribly I've bombed this thing.

The computer finally tells me that I've scored a whopping 16 percent. I'm kind of impressed that I even scored that high. I shut the computer down and step out into the hallway.

Besides a few wandering souls, the hallway is abandoned. A girl I don't recognize walks toward me. She's got basketball-shaped hall pass thing in her hand, and I see her turn toward the nurse's office. Just before she hits the door, she clutches her stomach and puts on a pained expression. Been there, done that. Pretending you're on your period to get out of class is probably the only advantage to living in the totally screwed-up world of the female reproductive cycle.

I climb the stairs toward Ms. Odum's class. With each step, I feel my heart rate skyrocketing, and by the time I reach her closed door, I feel like my chest is going to explode. I stop outside the portal to Hell. Most other doors in the school have some sort of cutesy signs or decorations. Those kinds of things, even the cheesy ones (here's looking at you, faded cartoon-cat-in-sunglasses-telling-me-that-reading-is-cool poster), have a way of taking the edge off a little bit.

But her door is a desert of old varnish. It's fitting, I suppose. Anything else would be a lie. Because on the other side of this bland, lifeless door is a land devoid of happiness and joy, an all-business, no-fun realm ruled by a dusty old grump with an iron grip and bad breath.

I grab the knob, half-expecting it to sizzle my hand, and turn it. I take a deep breath and begin loading up some angry smart-ass ammunition for the battle to follow.

But on the other side of the door is something that catches me completely off-guard and erases the cruel thoughts forming inside my head.

Ms. Odum is crying.

Chapter 10

SHE GIVES A little startle when I walk in. She clears her throat super loud a couple of times and sort of shuffles some papers around to look like she's been busy with teacher stuff and not with boo-hoooing at her desk. All that cover-up stuff just calls more attention to the fact that she's been crying about something.

I had this whole pissy-pants little speech worked up. You know, tell her where she can shove her stupid test and all that. But it flutters out the open window. I mean, I guess some part of me *knew* that there was a human being hidden somewhere under all that grumpy, hateful teachery stuff. But, to be honest, I never really thought the witch had any real non-evil feelings. It's like I just kind of assumed she was like one of those goofy carnival drawing things that I can't remember the name of. A *something-*ature with turned-down, bad-guy eyebrows and a permanent scowl.

It makes me wonder about all of the evil ladies in those old Disney movies. Did they have real feelings, too? When the cameras were off and no one was looking, did they cry, too? I'm blowing my own mind, here.

Steam hisses as I cool my overheated jets. "Oh...I...I'm sorry," I say, my voice sort of scared and stuttery. "I just...you told me to--"

"I know," she says. She waves my apology away with a hand clutching a soggy, wadded-up tissue. She tries to change the subject. "So how was your score?"

"Um...like, a 16," I say, still totally off balance. "Sorry." I wince a little as I spout out my pitiful score.

She sniffs again and blots her eyes. "Be honest with me. Did you even try?"

I weigh my options. Would it be worse to tell her the truth or to lie and say that I gave it the good old Randi try and still failed miserably. I opt for the truth this time. "No. Not really," I say. I pause for a second. "Well, not at all, actually."

She squeezes her eyes shut and turns her face away from me. Her shoulders bob up and down a little bit. She dabs at her face again.

My heart hurts to see this. What is going on? Do I really feel sorry for this mean old sack of bones? After all the crap she's given me? Why should I give a rat's fart about her?

But for some reason, I do care. Maybe there's still a little bit of a heart buried somewhere under all the ugly.

I give my head a "snap out of it" shake. That's it. There's only one explanation here. I fell asleep in that weird little room and woke up in an alternate dimension where my heartless beast of a math teacher actually has feelings. Either that or I'm just losing my freaking mind.

I take a couple of steps closer. I start to talk in this cautious whisper-voice like I'm afraid she's going to explode if I make too much noise. "Are...are you okay? Listen, if it means that much to you, I'll try harder next time. It's just...well...it's been a weird morning, that's all."

She turns and looks at me with crying eyes. Blue. I swear, if one more person cries on me today, I think I'm going to lose it for real. "It's not that, Dear," she says.

Dear? Dear!? What is going on? Is this the same lady that yells at me, like, every day? Oh, God. Now I know I'm a new permanent citizen of Bizarro World.

"But I do know that you could do much better than a 16 if you just tried," she says. "I know that you have a low opinion of yourself, but I believe that you might be surprised to find out what you are capable of if you only let go and really try." She takes a fresh tissue out of the box on her desk and gives a dainty little blow.

"What?" I ask. I'm hopelessly confused now.

"I had a conversation with Mr. Breckenridge about you, you know," she says. She sniffles, clears her throat, and straightens. "After the first day of school, he gave me a call and we spoke for a very long time."

"He did?" I ask. "What did he say?" It's hard to imagine the two of them having a real conversation with each other. I take a few cautious steps closer like I'm approaching an injured stray dog.

"He told me a lot, actually," she says. "He told me that you're one of the smartest kids that he's ever taught. He told me that you've been through a lot. He told me that you'd surprise me if I gave you a chance."

"He told you all that?"

She nods and wipes her eyes with a fresh tissue.

"Then why the heck have you still been so...so mean to me? You never even gave me a chance!" I feel Ugly Me clawing her way through to the surface again.

At this, fresh tears begin to flow down her wrinkled face. She squeezes her eyes closed and takes some deep breaths. "I know, Miranda," she says. She opens her eyes and looks down at her hands. "It hasn't always been like this."

"What do you mean?" I ask, a little sharpness creeping into my words.

"What I mean is that I used to be the kind of teacher that Mr. Breckenridge is. I used to be the one who all the kids loved. I used to have the energy and the drive and the passion." She sighs and looks at me. "But somewhere along the way, I became *this*. I never wanted to be the one that shouted and said hurtful things. I never wanted to be the old coot that made the students' lives miserable." As she speaks, her blue eyes lock onto mine, silently pleading for...for something I don't know how to give her. Ugly Me shrinks back.

"Well...then what happened?" I ask.

"Oh, I suppose it was a combination of things," she says. She gives a long sigh. "Not the least of which is that I've been doing this for thirty-two years now, you know."

A shocked expression plasters itself across my face. I don't even try to hide it. "Thirty-two years?" I say. My mouth hangs open for a second before I say anything else. "Jesus...that's, like, forever. I'd never last that long dealing with crazy kids like us. I'd snap after the first day. Like, for real. I'd murder someone."

When I say this, she does something I didn't think was possible: she smiles. Not a big, friendly grin or anything, but a shy little one that barely peeks out. It's almost like she's just learning how. "It can certainly be a challenge," she says, "but I do love my students."

I raise an eyebrow and put on a "yeah, right" face. "But you--"

"I know," she interrupts. "I know that I don't show it well, but--"

"*Ever*," I say.

She cracks another little smile and clears her throat. "I know that I don't show it *ever,* but I do. When I saw you today, *really* saw you, I remembered why I'm here."

"What do you mean?" I ask.

"You tripped because your shoe is broken. I'm not sure when it happened, but I know it has been that way for a while. It made me think about some other things that I've noticed. I have seen you taking extra food from the cafeteria. You wear the same clothes day after day. You shy away from most of the other students. You always look absolutely exhausted, but you especially do today," she says. She pauses for a second and tears up again. "You deserve so much more than what you've been given. And you deserve so much better than how I've treated you."

Her words rock me and strip me down to my bare bones. I feel like I've been punched in the gut. For a long, long time, I've tried so hard to coat myself in a thick crust of secrets and lies, but she has seen through it all. And if she's figured it out, then who else has? Am I really that transparent?

It's my turn to cry now.

Chapter 11

I DON'T KNOW if it's because I'm so exhausted or hungry or confused or hormonal or whatever, but the tears come fast and real and hard. They track down my cheeks like little warm rivers, and before I know it, I'm snotting and blubbering like a total wreck.

Ms. Odum stands up and presses a tissue into my hand. She puts her thin arm around me. Ugly Me, hurting and raw, wants me to get away. *Don't touch me!* But the tiny part of me still living inside shouts her down. I don't shrink back.

Her touch radiates warmth and comfort and peace. After all the stuff I've been through, these good things feel odd to me. They're an obscure foreign language that I used to speak but have long since forgotten. Locked away in my deep, dark insides are distant, blurry memories of this kind of thing. Warm hugs, laughter, kindness, sunshine.

But now, in the embrace of these bizarre circumstances, I feel like I've stepped out of my own body. I stand stiff and uncertain. I don't know whether I should break away from her or lean in and absorb all the rays of starshine I can.

I'm breaking. The tears come harder, and I can't stop them. Ugly Me curses me for being so weak and tries to dam the flow, but she has no power over me right now. The tears and strange feelings force her back and wear away the sharp edges inside me.

I cover my face with my scarred hands. Tears leak from beneath them. My legs turn to Jello and start to cave beneath me. I sink through quicksand and find myself on the floor, but she's still with me. She's on her knees beside me.

Both her arms wrap me up and pull me close. There's no impulse to flinch or fight or hurl hateful words. All that's left is this, a broken-down little me that craves so much of whatever this is.

Pity? Duty? Just plain love?

I don't care what it is.

I sink in, fully wrapped in the moment, truly warm for the first time in forever.

We stay that way for a minute. Me sitting on the floor, hands over my face, crying like a big, fat baby. Her kneeling next to me, holding me in her bony arms. My shoulders are bobbing up and down and my breath is coming in little shaky gasps. But even with that, I can feel her trembling, too. A tiny drop of wet weaves its way through my messy hair and touches my scalp, and I realize that she's crying even harder now than she was before.

She finally breaks the kind-of silence. "Look as us, Dear," she says. She gives one of those jittery "I've been crying like crazy" sighs. "We're just one big mess down here. Let's get out of this dirty floor," she says.

I sound a big, snotty snort and nod my head. I find my legs and stand up. She tries to stand with me, but she struggles to rise from her knees, grunting and making painful-sounding noises. I reach my hands down, and she takes them. I pull until she's on her feet. I help her limp back over to her worn-out desk chair. She sits down heavy with a little groan.

"Thank you," she says. "I'm afraid my legs just don't work like they used to."

I wipe my eyes on the sleeve of my recycled hoodie. "No," I say. "Thank you. I...I just don't know what to say. I--"

"Shhh," she says, cutting me off. "You don't have to say anything, Miranda. I'm the one who needs to talk now." She dabs at her eyes again and takes a deep breath. "I am sorry, truly sorry, for the way I have treated you. I've seen the signs all along, and Mr. Breckenridge even tried to tell me, but I still mistreated you." She breaks down crying again, big boo-hoos. "I am so sorry," she says again through the sobs.

I really don't know what to say. I'm used to getting crapped on, so I've got this whole arsenal of comebacks and nasty names and creative curses ready to go at a moment's notice. I'm like one of those crazy end-of-days prepper guys on T.V. Except instead of 50-gallon drums of rice and drinking water, I've squirreled away 101 creative and hurtful ways to say "screw you." But this apology totally disarms me and leaves me feeling naked and confused.

I can run. I can fight. I can hide. I can yell. I can curse.

But I don't know how to deal with *this*. I feel so stupid. Here I am, finally getting a taste of what I've been missing, and I'm standing here like a doofus.

"I...um...it's...it's okay," I finally manage to squeeze out.

"It really *isn't* okay, the way I've treated you," she says. "But thank you for saying that." She blows her nose. Then she gives me a little smile. The bright white fluorescent lights dance over her wet eyes and create little dots of starlight.

It occurs to me again that I never thought of her as a whole person before. To me, she was always just the mean old coot of a teacher, nothing beyond the surface except more layers of teacher stuff. I know what she means when she said that thing about really *seeing* me.

I'm really *seeing* her now, and it feels like I'm looking into a mirror. Ms. Odum isn't a heartless beast any more than I am. She definitely has a heart under all that hard teacher/grownup stuff. Fresh tears swell in my eyes.

Yes. She has a heart. And so much like mine, her heart has been locked away, bound up by hurts and nearly forgotten.

I have no words to say. My body speaks. I walk over, my heart finally unbound and remembered.

I place my arms around her.

The tears flow.

Chapter 12

SILENCE RULES AGAIN. This time, my mind doesn't search for ways to fill the silence. Instead, I allow myself to fall deep into the warmth creeping into my long-frozen limbs. I savor the moment and breathe the happy in deep and long.

The speaker on the wall crackles to life and brings us back. "Ms. Odum?" says the voice of Ms. Joan.

Ms. Odum sniffs, clears her throat, and answers. "Yes?"

"Your delivery is in the office. Would you like me to send someone up with it?" asks the disembodied voice.

"No, thank you," Ms. Odum says. "I'll come down and get it."

"Alright," says Ms. Joan. The speaker clicks and goes silent.

Ms. Odum grabs a fresh tissue and stands. She walks to the door, still limping from being on the floor with me.

"Do you need some help?" I ask.

"No, thank you, Dear," she says. "But I would like for you to stay here and wait for me to return."

"But I really should--"

"I've already let your other teachers know that you're with me. Please stay here." With this, she gives a curt little nod and leaves the room. She closes the door behind her. I wonder if that's a request or a command.

Am I a guest here or a prisoner?

I look at the clock on the wall. This has been the weirdest morning of my life, and I have this sneaking suspicion that it's about to get even weirder. I try to think of how it could possibly get more bizarre, but aside from, like, an alien invasion or something, I can't think of anything that would rock my little boat harder than it's already been rocked.

I stare around the room. I've never really bothered to look around here that much. When I'm here for class, I usually just stare hate rays at the wall or sit like a lump and put my head on my desk until Ms. Odum sends me out of class. This is a whole new perspective for me.

She's got a line of plants on the long windowsill in the back of the room. They're all different, but they all look sort of similar at the same time. All the plants are kind of squatty-looking and are covered in these leaf-but-not-quite-leaf things of all different shapes. They're all different shades of green, but some of them have this kind of reddish tinge to them, like they're wearing lipstick or something. The leaf-things all sort of have this bloated look to them like they'd burst if you squeezed them. I'm pretty sure there's a name for that kind of plant, but I can't think of it right now.

The plants are actually really pretty in this haphazard sort of way. There's a ton of them, and not that I'm an expert or anything, but they all look very healthy. They don't spill out of their containers loaded with years of hairy-looking weeds like the couple of broken pots at my house. She must spend a lot of time caring for these things. There's a miniature watering can at the end of the row of plants, and I picture her walking to the water fountain and back a zillion times a day just to water all these plants.

I plop down in a desk and stare at the plants. When I was little, we had this old neighbor lady who had a flower garden in her front yard. I remember seeing her totter around and fuss over it for what seemed like hours a day. She wore this worn-out old dress with faded flower print. She cared for those flowers like they were her children. Stooping down and pulling the weeds that threatened them. Cooing and talking to the fresh little buds. Covering them with old blankets and sheets of plastic when the weather got cold.

In the springtime, when the gray memories of winter chill still clung to the air, these amazing yellow flowers would pop up.

They'd dot the beds with splashes of bright sunshine and light up the whole block. I loved those things.

I was either too young or too shy or too scared to ever talk to the lady, but she saw me looking at the yellow flowers one day. Maybe she saw something in the way I looked at them because she came out with little scissor things and clipped a handful of them. She walked over and handed them to me, a thin bouquet of long-stemmed sunlight.

"Daffodils," she said. She smiled at me. "They're my favorite. Take them inside and put them in some water. They'll brighten the whole room."

I don't remember saying anything to the lady, but I do remember those flowers. Mom put them in a tall, clear glass of water on the kitchen counter. I remember the way they seemed to light up. I remember how mom smiled.

I also remember how I cried when Mom got angry and threw the glass at Dad when he came in late. I remember walking into the kitchen in the morning and seeing the daffodils wilting on the floor among the broken shards. I scooped them up and tried to revive them with fresh water. They perked up a little, but they never got their sunshine back.

Not long after that, all the brightness and color started to bleed out of my world in little bits and pieces.

Back in the spring, Mom and I had a huge fight. She kicked me out of the house, and I had nothing to do but wander around the city all day. *Shivering.* It was one of those cold early spring days where the sun just teases but doesn't warm. I don't know how it happened, but I somehow found my old house. I suppose my feet remembered. The old neighbor lady's house was gone, but in the vacant lot left behind, a little row of fresh daffodils bloomed in the overgrown grass. I couldn't believe it. After all this time, these things were still here, digging themselves out of the cold dirt every spring. Bringing brightness and memories to the world.

I waded through the weeds and broke a couple of them away from the ground. I took them home and sat them on the table with a little note. "I'm sorry, Mom," it said. I don't remember what I was sorry about or if I had even done anything wrong. Most likely, I was just trying to appease Mount Mom, always spewing lava for no reason at all.

The daffodils wilted and died on the table, untouched.

I dig deep in my tired brain for a word I learned in science class for those plants who hang on through the wintertime, dug in deep and sleeping the cold away, clawing their way through the dirt to bloom again in the warmer times.

Perennial.

When will I claw my way out of the frozen dirt of my wintertime? Will I ever? Is there another version of me lying dormant beneath the Ugly? Beneath the cold that has spread over my life and killed all the good and bright things?

Will I ever bloom again? Is there a fresh version of me somewhere dressed in bright living colors?

A Perennial Girl?

I hear a god-awful commotion on the other side of the door. The knob rattles, and the sounds of grunting and clattering objects leaks in from under the doorway. The knob rattles a little more, and the door creaks open.

Ms. Odum shuffles through the doorway, and my mouth hits the floor.

Chapter 13

SHE COMES THROUGH the door, one hand on the knob, the other balancing a pizza box. A few paper plates litter the floor behind her. They must have hit the floor while she was fiddling with the door. She smiles at me as she enters the room.

"Are you hungry?" she asks. Her eyes are alight.

"Yes!" I say. A huge grin spreads across my face before I can even feel it coming. It's totally involuntary, and I can't even begin to try to conceal it. Fueled by pure happy.

I again feel so bare and vulnerable, but I'm starting to be fine with that.

"You like pizza, right? I wanted to surprise you, so I ordered something that I was fairly certain you'd enjoy."

Tears fill my eyes. I can't speak.

Her smile melts down. She wrinkles her forehead. "You don't like it, then? I'm sorry, I--"

"No," I cut her off with a little more sharpness than I intend. We're both shocked into a brief silence. "I...I love it," I say. Her smile perks back up. "I mean...I like pizza, but...I love...," I wave my hand around, sweeping in the smiling woman, the food, the row of plants in the window--everything. I swallow hard and force back more tears. "I love *this*." I feel warmth drip down my cheek.

Her eyes glisten with new wet. She sighs deep. "Me, too," she says. "It's been such a long time."

"Yeah," I say. "It has been for me, too."

She bends down and tries to scoop up the paper plates while

still holding the pizza. She loses her balance and teeters a little. I rush over and steady her.

"Let me get those," I say. Before she can protest, I grab the plates and close the door. I don't want any intruders to creep in and steal this moment away from me.

She puts the pizza on a desk and flips open the top. The smell fills the room, and I'm afraid that I'm going to start drooling like a dog. Pepperoni and sausage. It's a thing of beauty.

"Well, help yourself," she says. She gestures toward the open box. "We don't have a lot of time."

I take two slices and begin stuffing my face. Ms. Odum takes a slice and begins to chew, too. The world kind of disappears as I focus on shoveling it in. I can't remember the last time I tasted something so amazing. I've been relegated to school cafeteria food and scraps for so long.

At some point, I come up for air and realize that she's staring at me as she chews. She's got this sort-of smile on her face, but I can see a shadow of concern behind it.

I swallow hard. "Sorry," I say. "I don't mean to be such a pig."

"No need to apologize, Dear," she says. "I'm just glad you're enjoying it."

I nod and grab another slice. "Thank you so much," I say. "This is amazing. Seriously."

She smiles and nods. "You're welcome. I'm happy to be here with you."

The lunch bell cuts through the air. The hallway on the other side of the door begins to fill with loud voices. I go to stand up, but she puts her hand on my arm. "You can stay here if you want to," she says.

"Oh...okay," I say. "I don't want to take up all your time, though."

"Please," she says. "I haven't enjoyed being here like this in a long time. You're not *taking up* anything." She looks down at her plate. "You've given me so much today."

"What do you mean?" I ask. Not that I've been keeping score or anything, but the only thing I've given her today is another terrible test score for her permanent teacher record.

"Things have been very difficult for me since I lost Charles." She reaches over and picks up a framed photo from her desk. In it, I see a younger Ms. Odum standing knee-deep in the ocean, her pants pulled up to her thighs. She's bent-over pulling some kind of basket thing out of the water. Kneeling next to her in the water is a handsome man in a wide-brimmed hat. He's helping her haul the basket out of the water. They're both looking at the camera and smiling pure happy. She stares down at the photo and caresses it with her thumb. "It was just the two of us for 42 years. He died a little over a year ago, and it has been so hard to find anything to smile about."

"I'm so sorry," I say. It's really hard for me to imagine being with anyone for that long. Of course, my options right now are limited to the awkward, zitty goofballs that wander the halls of the school playing bloody knuckles and giving each other wedgies, so I don't have much to go on. But if I was with someone for that long, I'd probably just pull a Juliet the second they died. Not that anyone could ever stand me for longer than two seconds.

I definitely can't blame her for being such a miserable grump. I think about all the crap I've given her. I feel a pit forming in my stomach as I recount all of the snippy, immature, grumpy-butt bull I've thrown her way over the last few weeks.

I used to hear kids talk about her, so ever since before I even met her, I thought she was just this rude, mean old teacher who deserved whatever bullshit I threw at her. All along, though, she's been a hurting, lonely, exhausted human being who needed something sunny and warm to bring her back to life.

Just like me.

My next thought punches me in the pizza-loaded gut and takes my breath away.

I'm not alone.

I think about all the miserable, mean, ugly people around me. Headband Girl and her gang. The kids who call me names. The teachers who give me *that* look when I show my face in class. Random jerks on the street.

All this time, I had convinced myself that I was some piece of

ugly garbage, floating along like pollution in a crystal-clear sea.
But now I wonder just how different I really am.

Chapter 14

NEITHER OF US says much after that. I guess we're just kind of soaking it all in, basking in whatever this is. It's not an awkward silence at all, though. Before today, I would have gouged my eyes out with a rusty spoon if someone told me that I'd have to spend more than five seconds alone in a room with Ms. Odum.

This whole situation covers me like a warm quilt, and with a finally-full stomach, I'm a goner in no time. I don't wake up until I feel Ms. Odum shaking me and calling my name. I slept right through the bell.

I shake the sleep out of my eyes. Ms. Odum laughs and wipes at my cheek with a tissue. It comes away red. My eyes go wide and I begin to enter freak-out mode.

She sees the wild look in my eyes and laughs again. "Pizza sauce," she says. She nods down at the plate in front of me. A smashed, half-eaten slice stares back at me.

I must have passed out mid-bite.

I yawn and stretch like a satisfied cat. "I'm sorry," I say. "I wasn't trying to be rude. I--"

"Don't worry, Dear," she says. "You must be absolutely exhausted to just go out like that."

"You have no idea," I say. I take a few tissues and go to work on the side of my face. I think I even have sauce in my ear.

"It's time for my next class, but I need you to do something for me before you report to yours."

"Okay," I say.

She hands me a sealed envelope. "Take this down to the nurse.

Stay there while she reads it."

"Um...okay," I say. I raise a suspicious eyebrow, but she doesn't respond.

The hallway beyond the door begins to get crowded with voices waiting to come inside. Loud ones. It's the customary post-lunch high, and I swear it sounds like the kids out there are screaming their heads off. Again, I don't know how any human being could stand to work a job in a school full of these crazy people. I'd be so depressed if I knew that my college degree was being spent on teaching hormonal nutcases how to write complete sentences while trying to keep emotionally-unstable kids from getting into fistfights over stupid crap like which YouTuber is best or whether or not a hotdog is considered a sandwich.

It sounds crazy, but both of those things have actually happened.

"Go on, now," she says and shoos me toward the door. She stashes the leftovers in her tall teacher cabinet thing and turns to face me again.

"Thank you," I say. "Thank you for everything."

"It was truly my pleasure," she says with a smile.

I leave the room and wade through the crowd. My standard move these days is to keep my eyes pointed at the dirty floor tiles and walk fast. It's easier to ignore the ugly looks and secret little giggles that way. The hallway is super crowded, so my going is slow. But even with my eyes firmly fixed on the crowd's shoes, I can hear the little comments. It's a stormy sea of hateful voices.

"What was *she* doing in there?"

"Probably trying to murder Ms. Odum or something."

"Do you smell something?"

"Ugh! She ever heard of a washing machine?"

As each little comment hits me, I feel the good vibes chipping away. A cold fog settles on whatever just happened with me and Ms. Odum. I try to ignore it all and find my way back, but I get lost in the thick, choking hate around me.

"Such a *freak.*"

I soldier on like a good little girl, not responding, trying to pretend that I don't hear. Trying to hold my head high while staring at the floor.

"Looks like she spent the night in a dumpster."

I hug my arms tight around myself. I begin to tremble as I struggle to swallow down whatever it is that's straining to come out of me. I don't know what I want to say or do right now, but I know that I don't want to see it.

"What is *wrong* with her?"

The tears come. I feel them on my cheeks. These aren't the same ones I cried with Ms. Odum. They sting and burn. The old tears are back again.

So, so soon.

Why did I think, even for a second, that things were going to be okay?

"Is *that* the one you were talking about?"

I make the mistake of glancing up just in time to see Headband Girl and her little gang of perfumed sheep. When she sees me, she pinches her nose and scrunches up her stupid too-much-makeup-wearing face like she smells something rotten. Giggles ripple through the entire group of girls. They cover their mouths with fingernails painted in matching aqua blue paint. But those pretty nails can't hide the ugly.

Before I know what's happening, and before I can even hope to stop it, Ugly Me jumps into action.

Chapter 15

MY LITTLE WORLD goes black, and I'm no longer me.

"Leave me alone, you bitch!" I scream. I launch myself at her and grab her by that stupid blonde ponytail. I'm no longer a seventh-grade girl. I'm a desperate wild animal, punching and scratching and clawing.

We end up on the floor. I'm on top, slapping and punching and cursing. She's under me, shielding her face, sobbing. Her friends try to pull me off, but I swat them away. They back off and scatter like dead leaves in the wind.

They were happy to giggle and whisper along with her before, but they want no part of this.

I feel big, strong hands lift me away. They hold me firm, but I flail and kick against them, trying to get back to my prey, hungry for more. I'm cranked-up on all kinds of anger and adrenaline, but my tiny self is no match for the hands holding me. I sure give them a run for their money, though.

I'm dragged away from Headband Girl, who is now standing and crying into some teacher's arms. The world comes back into focus, and I see the faces around me. They're laughing and smiling. Some of them are applauding and punching the air. A few of them have their phones pointed toward me.

Teachers yell for everyone to get their butts to class. Kids begin to disappear into classrooms. Show's over. But the damage is done. It'll be all over the Internet by now, for the amusement of all posterity.

Randi Lewis, Dumpster Girl, is a crazy psycho nutcase. Stay

away. Stay very far away.

I stop struggling. Whatever gusto I gained from the pizza and the nap is sucked right out of me. My legs go numb, but the strong hands keep me from falling. I look up at my captor. He's some teacher-man that I don't know. He doesn't say anything. He's breathing hard and shaking a little bit. His face is all red and sweaty. I hang my head and allow myself to be dragged to the office.

I plop down in the hotseat outside the principal's office. This whole situation is all too familiar. I swear there's a dent in this seat the exact shape of my bony butt. I fit right in down here with the troublemakers and school rejects.

I give myself another internal slap to the face for being foolish enough to think that something good was happening here. I let my guard down, I let someone in, and now look where I am.

Stupid girl. There's no room in my life for anything but *this*.

I can't believe I tried to fool myself into thinking that there was any non-ugly, non-miserable version of me left inside after all this time. I'm not a dormant flower. I'm a living dead girl, hollow and rotten inside. Allergic to happiness.

I hear a commotion and look down the little office suite hall and see Headband Girl being led into the nurse's office. Her hair's a ginormous mess, and she's covering her face and sobbing some major big boo-hoos. She's really pouring herself into the performance, big hysterical gasps and everything.

"What happened?" asks the nurse. She coos like a new mother.

It takes Headband Girl a while to calm down enough to answer. "She...attacked me...for no reason!" she finally manages to squeeze out through the sobbing fits.

No reason. No reason, my fat hairy toe. I wonder if they'll buy that load of raw sewage. Not that it matters. I've been here enough times to know that when it comes to these situations, it's the kids like me who are the bad guys. Might as well lock me up and throw away the key. No trial, no mercy.

Because it's not against the rules to be a gargantuan asshole, but the second the claws come out, the authorities suddenly take an interest.

I get it, I guess. I can't go around going all nutso on anyone who pisses me off. Peace and love and public safety and all that. Plus, I'd get myself killed or locked up in no time flat.

Mr. B would always tell me that it was okay to stand up for myself. It just wasn't cool to beat the crap out of people. That's fine and all, but in my world, fighting and screaming and cursing are necessary life skills best learned early and practiced often.

I have no clue how to deal with crap like this any other way. Add that to the long list of reasons that a girl like me doesn't belong in a place like this.

I wish there was a special school for dirty, no-social-skills-having losers like me.

The door to the principal's office swings open. I look up, expecting to see the familiar, perpetually-exhausted face of Mr. Gorley. But it's not him. It's some gray-headed guy with a buttload of serious frown lines beaten into his wrinkled face. No doubt he's some poor sucker brought out of retirement to fill in for Mr. Gorley. His facial expression is icy cold. He's probably pissed because he could be playing golf or fishing right now but instead has to deal with me.

I follow him inside and take a seat. There's a bookmarked spy novel on the desk. Great. I also interrupted his afternoon reading. This is going to go well.

He clears his throat. "So--"

"Let's just make this quick," I interrupt. "I know you don't want to deal with this, so just tell me how long I'm suspended and I'll be on my way." I feel like a deflated balloon.

He chuckles. "Straight to the point, huh? I respect that," he says. He types a couple of words on the computer in front of him. It takes him forever. He uses two crooked index fingers and stalks each individual letter before smashing it.

He squints at the screen. "Looks like three days for fighting," he says.

"Sounds about right," I say. Been here, done this.

"Well, do you need to hear a speech?" he asks. "Or should I skip that, too."

"You can skip it," I say. "I've heard all the speeches before, but here I still am."

"Well, then. Maybe it's not speeches you need," he says. He looks away from the screen and locks eyes with me.

"I break eye contact and stare at my filthy jeans. I sigh. "I don't know what I need, but I sure as hell know I haven't found it here," I say. Silence falls.

"Are you sorry?" he asks, changing the subject.

The question catches me off-guard. Am I sorry? If I'm being honest, the thing I'm most sorry about is having to fend for myself for three whole days. In fact, I try not to think of that. The thought alone threatens to send me into panic freakout mode. But am I sorry about what I did? That's a tricky question.

"I hope she's not hurt," I say after a long pause. "I really don't want to hurt anybody. I just want people to leave me alone." I pause again and look out the window. There's this big tree outside. A couple of squirrels are going bonkers out on a limb. "But no, I'm not really sorry."

"Fair enough," he says. He gives another little chuckle. He squints at the computer again and picks up the phone. "Well, let's call your mom and get this over with."

Good luck with that. My mom has had, like, five numbers in the past year, and she hasn't filled out any paperwork for the school since the beginning of last year when she went through this "I'm going to get my shit together and start acting like a real mom" phase.

I think that one lasted three days.

He dials a number. I hear a faint echo of a harsh tone and a computerized voice. He frowns and clicks a couple of things on the computer screen. He dials another number. A very confused person on the other end of the line tells him he's got the wrong number.

A few more clicks, another dialed number, another error message.

Welcome to my world, Bub. Before my phone was stolen from me by some random freak-o, I could sometimes get in touch with my mom on whatever social media she was posting embarrassing pictures on that day. But that was only if I was lucky and she was in the right mood.

I've pretty much learned to accept the fact that in my world, I'm the only one I can rely on.

He hangs up the phone and looks over at me. "Do you know how to get in touch with your mom?" he asks.

I shake my head. "But it's okay," I add. "I can just show myself out. I'll tell her what's going on." I'm already wracking my brain for how I'll spend the next three days. Staying at home is out of the question. No way Mom will let me hang around while she's doing whatever the heck she does during the day with whoever the heck hangs out with her. She'll kick me out for sure.

Besides, I've been trapped in this routine long enough to know that I'm better off on my own, wandering the city like some stray puppy, pretending to be invisible.

He sighs. "I wouldn't feel good about letting you walk home," he says. "Are you sure you can't get in touch with your mother?"

"Seriously, it's okay," I say. "I'll be fine. I walk all the time. Just ask anyone."

He picks up the phone and presses a button. I hear the voice of Ms. Joan on the other line. She confirms that, in fact, my mom is a loser and that I'm basically a feral child who's just going to walk where I want to, anyway. Bless my little heart.

"Okay," he says as he hangs up the phone. "I guess you can go. But just be careful, okay? I'm coming back in a couple of weeks, and I'd like it if you were still here."

I nod and stand up. He's not bad, this one. At least he didn't yell at me.

I stare at the floor as I leave the office and head to the door. I don't want to look anyone else in the eyes. As I put distance between me and the school, my heart starts to pound as a feeling of panic grips me tight. Familiar questions float around in my exhausted mind.

What am I going to eat?

Where will I go?

What is my mom going to do to me if she finds out I'm suspended and have to stay home?

My feet keep moving as my mind races. Before I bombed the

math test, I'd somehow finagled the tape on my shoe to sort-of hold again, but it totally gives up the ghost out here on the rough sidewalk. The sole on my shoe flops loose again, a constant tripping hazard. I walk on, trying to reassure myself that I can survive this.

But just as I begin to calm down, another thought pops up and steals my breath.

Hard metal against my cheek. Whispered threats.

Now I'm really panicking.

Chapter 16

THE SCHOOL ISN'T too far away. I could just go back, ring the bell, and spill the beans about the whole break-in situation. But at the same time, the thought of setting foot back into that place right now seems laughable. Besides, the tender little bruise on my cheek reminds me of what's at stake.

If I tell and the cops show up at my house, they'll kill me and my mom. They've obviously been watching my house, so they'll definitely notice the cops sniffing around. And as soon as it gets dark, we'll be sitting ducks.

I walk on, putting distance between myself and the school. Just before I turn the corner, I look back at the building. Dark clouds roll in and cast dim shadows across the school's enormous white columns. As much as I hate that place right now, it's definitely much safer than anywhere else I can think of.

I'm tempted again to turn around and take my busted shoe back there. But I've just been given a very clear message.

You're not welcome here. Come back and try again soon. Better luck next time, you big, fat screw-up.

Once again, I've been chewed up and spit out like old bubblegum. I can't go back to where I don't belong. I turn the corner, leaving the school behind. I have to walk in this weird, uncomfortable way because my broken shoe threatens to trip me anytime there's the slightest bump or obstacle. I slog along in this kind of half-march, and before I've gone too far, my shin starts to burn like fire. I might be better off to just take the darn shoe off, but I've seen way too many old needles and broken bottles. I'd rather deal with a sore leg than some horrible disease.

I hear a distant rumble. The clouds are getting thicker, rolling in all fat and gray and grumpy-looking. Great. Let's just top this whole hellish day off by getting stuck in a thunderstorm. I don't so much mind getting wet. It might even wash some of my stink away. Not that I can smell myself anymore, but I know that other people can. I try to stay as clean as I can, but when my mom doesn't pay the bills or buy soap or laundry detergent, it's really hard.

I can get used to my own stench, but I can't get used to the way people wrinkle their noses or scootch away when I'm near. To be fair, most people don't do it to be mean, but it still pricks me every time. And those little pinpricks of pain add up to big, nasty hurts.

I can deal with the rain. I'm used to being uncomfortable. But I hate the thunder and lightning. Always have. I don't know what it is, but when the storms come, I totally lose it in this crazy, uncontrollable way. My big girl brain knows that I'll be fine as long as I'm not standing outside like an idiot, but some small, scared part of me takes control when the lights and sounds come.

Back when I had some sort of real life, Daddy would protect me from the storms. I could run and hide in his arms, and his smell and his voice and his warm would scare away the loudest, brightest storms. In that life, I would sleep like a baby in his arms, safe from anything or anyone.

But now, I have nowhere to hide. The roof protects my shivering body from the lightning, but I have no warm, safe set of arms to run to anymore. When the storms come, I cower, scared and alone, shaking for hours even after the noises and lights are gone.

The sky booms again. My little ticker starts to pound double-time. I walk faster, not caring that I trip, like, every five steps. I hadn't planned on going home so soon. I was content with wandering aimlessly and stewing in my own misery until I thought of something better to do or was too tired to walk any more. But this changes everything. There's nothing at home for me but fear and pain. But at least it's familiar. Uncomfortable is my comfort zone now, and I'd rather be there once the storm hits.

It wouldn't do for me to totally lose it in the open air. At home I can at least curl up and be miserable, but I'm afraid of what I might do out here.

The sky shouts again, a bit closer this time. I pick up my pace. My shoe catches on a big crack in the sidewalk, and I stumble. I flail around and try to catch my balance, but it's no use. I fall hard. My hands break my fall, and I feel fire in my palms against the pavement. More thunder. I scramble back to my feet and look at my palms while I walk.

No blood this time, but my hands are scuffed up pretty bad. White and pink lines streak my palms. They burn. More thunder. I move faster. I break into an almost-run, doing a high-knee with my broken shoe. I must look insane, but I don't care. I just need to move.

I take the shortcuts today, even though they track through the scary neighborhoods. The breeze turns into a steady wind. Porch-sitters shoo their kids inside and lower their threadbare umbrellas and cover their beat-up chairs. There's no sign of the guy with the weird head. Thank God for that. I don't know why, but I'm more afraid of the storm than I am of the crazy people.

More thunder. Louder. Closer.

I run.

My awkward gait exhausts my leg and makes my muscles burn. But I don't care.

I run.

The sole of my shoe catches on the sidewalk again. But this time, I don't fall. Instead, the hard rubber outsole rips clean off. It bounces into some scraggly bushes, but I don't stop to look for it. All that's left to protect the bottom of my foot is a dirty sock and the thin, worn-out canvas insole.

I run.

Every tiny rock and piece of garbage digs into my foot now. It hurts, but I don't care.

I run.

Wind. Rain now. Thunder shakes the world. Too close.

I run.

Something sharp breaks through the dead shoe and hurts me. I'm probably bleeding, but I don't stop to look.

Harder rain. Thunder so loud I cover my ears. Lightning blinds me. My heart pounds big panic thumps against my ribs.

I run.

I see the yellow sign of the dollar store ahead. It's not home, but it'll have to do. I don't know how much longer I can make it out here. Maybe Vulture Lady will fold me into her wings.

The rain soaks me to the skin. I open the door and fling myself inside.

I take a deep, shaky breath and look up.

I see who's standing at the counter.

My heart stops.

I run back into the storm.

Chapter 17

I DON'T HEAR the thunder anymore. I can't feel the rain. The flashes of blinding light no longer register in my brain.

All I can see are those blue eyes.

I thought my heart was racing before, but now I can feel it throbbing throughout my whole body. I'm trembling all over, shaking so hard that my teeth chatter together and threaten to break apart. I walk toward home in a daze.

He looks *different* now. Changed. The messy brown hair, the stuff I used to run my little fingers through, is gone, scraped away with sharp edges like everything else good in my life. The soft, kind face I remember is marked up with rough and ugly inks. The years morphed him into some kind of shadow creature with blue eyes sunk deep within. He no longer matches the pictures in my head that play over and over again. But I remember those eyes.

My dad's eyes.

Did he see me? If he did, would he even recognize me?

In my shattered mind, I rewind and play the whole scene back. My dad's eyes in a stranger's head, buying cigarettes at the store. Two other men I don't recognize standing next to him. Explosions in my head, my brain melting into terror goo. Me, running back into the storm.

My head struggles to comprehend.

Dad is back.

Back when he was first sent away, I longed for this moment. I prayed every night that God would send my daddy back to me. I prayed the Lord my soul to keep and for my little life to begin again, full of Mom and Dad happy and love.

I prayed those little kid prayers for years until I could no longer force myself to believe that there was even a tiny shred of hope that my old life could come back. My hope was lost, buried and crushed beneath the weight of pain and sadness and fear.

In my prayers and hopes, I pictured Daddy coming home like he used to. He'd be tired from hard work, but that wouldn't stop him from picking me up and tossing me in the air. We'd laugh and smile and be happy and in love.

That's how I used to think it could be again some day. But now that the someday is in the here and now, I'm confused and terrified and sick.

So many questions.

How long has he been out?

Why hasn't he tried to see me?

Is he even supposed to be here?

Why didn't anyone tell me?

Does Mom know?

Who were those people with him?

Will he try to find me?

If he finds me, what will he do?

My breath starts to come in quick, ragged gasps. The ground rises to meet me, hard and cold. My chest feels tight. Am I having a heart attack? What is happening?

I lie on the sidewalk in the storm, a broken girl, struggling to catch my breath. I'd call out for help, but I can't make a sound. Even if I could, I don't think anyone would come. Who would want to help something like me?

I don't know how long it takes, but I'm finally able to catch my breath. I curl my knees into my chest and hug them tight against me. I rock back and forth on the wet sidewalk, my tears mingling with the rain.

My mind is a jumble. I think I'm going insane. Then one image from the store flashes into my brain and slaps me in the face. I stop rocking and jump to my feet.

In the store, one of the men with my dad. Long hair and a

white tank top.

Last night, a strange man on the sidewalk. Two intruders sent by someone else.

I sprint toward my house.

I have to warn Mom.

Chapter 18

I POUND DOWN the wet sidewalk. My foot hurts. I feel the cut opening farther. Every other step is a fresh new agony. I risk a glance behind me and see little puddles of red spreading on the concrete. My body screams at me to stop, but I press on.

There will be time to bleed and cry later. I can't stop now.

A car I don't recognize splashes past me, spraying me with dirty street water. Ahead, I see it turn down my street. I run-limp to the corner and stop. What I see makes me sick. The strange car is parked on the street in front of my house. The brake lights glow red and little clouds of exhaust wheeze out of the rusty tailpipe. They've left it running. Even from almost a block away, I can tell that my front door is half-open. Beyond it, the house is dark.

It's too late it's too late it's too late!

I stop and crouch down behind a scraggly row of bushes in someone's yard. I watch while my heart tries to leap out of my throat. No movement, no lights inside. The car idles out front. My breath comes out in little puffs in time with my erratic heartbeats.

Maybe it's nothing. Maybe it isn't them. Mom has all kinds of freaky visitors all the time. It could all be just a coincidence. Maybe I'm just freaking out for no reason.

But some wise little part of me deep inside tells me that this whole situation definitely isn't right. The little voice tells me to be careful. Don't do anything stupid.

I watch for a few more minutes. I can hear my heart pumping

in my ears. Still nothing. The windows are dark. The car hasn't moved.

The storm has passed over. The thunder and lightning disappear into the distance, leaving behind a blanket of light gray across the sky. A fine mist of rain clings to the air around me. I stand up and tiptoe toward the house. My foot protests, but I can't just sit here and do nothing.

I think about banging on a neighbor's door and calling the cops. But what would I say? Nothing has happened even though my mythical female danger senses are tingling like mad crazy. I'm pretty sure there's not a police code for a girl with a serious case of the willies.

I touch my cheek, still tender from last night's intrusion. I haven't forgotten those words.

I can't risk it. I'm on my own, just like always.

The world is all silence and painful tension. The storm has chased away the usual daytime sounds. The air is heavy. I approach the house, wound tight and ready to spring. A dog barks somewhere near me, and I almost jump out of my soggy clothes. I'm only a few yards away from the house when I hear the shouting.

The sounds cut through the silence and make me flinch. I freeze. I can't understand what they're saying, but they fill my frazzled brain with terror. I'm glued to the spot, my feet refusing to obey my commands to run, to hide, to get help, to do *something* other than just stand here all scared and useless.

My ears pick a woman's voice out of the jumble. Mom. Her voice is shrill and angry-scared. Two men trade shouts. I pick out a handful of curses, but I still can't understand the rest. I'm a useless statue, worn-out and crumbling.

The voices crescendo into a roar of shouts and screams and curses. A loud *pop pop pop*. Three orange flashes of light in the window. My mom's scream, terrified.

A man runs out of the house, clutching his shoulder. Streaks of growing red stain a white tank top. He stumbles hard into the side of the car. He scrabbles at the door handle, opens it, and jumps in. The tires screech as the car speeds away.

More shouts and screams. More flashes and loud sounds. Glass shatters. Distant sirens wail.

I'm doing a panic dance, pacing around and pulling on my hair. My mind is gone. I have no more thoughts. Only dark fear.

Police cars roar by with blue lights and sirens, but I barely hear them. My ears are filled with cotton now. The world is muffled and distant. My knees buckle and send me back down to the wet sidewalk.

Officers crouch behind their cars with guns drawn. They take aim and shout at the front door. They all yell at once, deep voices thick with testosterone and fear and adrenaline. A skeleton with my mother's face runs out of the house with her hands in the air. Her elbows bulge on twig-like arms. There are small splotches of blood on the pajamas hanging loose and baggy over her sickly frame.

I barely recognize her. When did she get like this?

She approaches the officers. They yell more, and she stumbles to her knees, hands still in the air. One officer breaks away and shoves her down onto the muddy lawn. A few seconds pass, then Mom is dragged to her feet. Blue flashes reflect off of the silver handcuffs that now bind her hands. She disappears into one of the cruisers.

I finally come alive and run toward the car. "Mom!" I yell. "Mom!"

As I run nearer, I hear voices calling to me, saying things that I either don't understand or just ignore. I make it to the car holding her, but big strong arms grab me and keep me from grabbing the handle. For the second time today, I flail and struggle like a trapped animal, spitting and cursing while the world blacks out around me.

A familiar word breaks through the darkness.

"Miranda?" it says.

I stop struggling and look around. The owner of the voice approaches, his face wearing a look of surprise and concern. His pistol, still in his hand, is pointed at the ground. His nameplate flashes in the blue lights.

Anderson.

The world comes back into focus. Our eyes meet, but I have no words.

"Miranda!" he says, still in disbelief that I'm here. I stop struggling against the hands holding me. "Let her go, Chuck," he says to my captor.

The hands relax their hold. Officer Anderson holsters his gun and takes a few steps toward me. "Are you okay?" he asks.

I nod. "My mom...is she hurt? I saw blood. What's happening?"

He motions to the closed cruiser door. "Is *she* your mom?"

I nod again.

He steps closer and reaches out to me. "I don't think she's hurt. The blood is someone else's, I think," he says. "But listen, Miranda." He pauses, struggling to find the right words. "She's in a lot of trouble. We've been after her for a while." He sighs. "She's been involved in a lot of bad stuff." He looks down at his muddy boots. "I'm sorry."

A commotion in front of the house steals our attention. The man who used to be my father is standing in the mud, cursing at the officers.

"Hands in the air!" says someone.

"On the ground! Now!" says someone else.

An officer is approaching him from the side, but he's too focused on screaming at the others.

"I said get on the ground!"

Before he can respond, he's tackled from the side. More curses, more yelling. I fall into Officer Anderson's arms and bury my face into his rough shirt. I can't bear to watch. He puts a warm hand over my ear to deaden the sounds. He squeezes me tight.

More fighting. More screaming. I'm losing my mind. A soft *pop*, then a string of loud, rapid clicking sounds. My dad's angry shouts turn to screams of pain.

"Give me your hands, or we'll give it to you again!"

He responds with a defiant curse.

More clicking noises, more pained shouts, then silence.

I extract my face and look toward the house. He's being dragged to his feet, hands cuffed. The barbs from the taser are hanging from his chest.

Our eyes meet. I see, once again, those blue eyes that I used to love. I see, once again, those blue eyes disappear into the back of a police car.

It's all too much for my exhausted mind.

All at once, the lights go out.

Chapter 19

I WAKE UP in the back of an ambulance when a paramedic sticks one of those horrible-smelling ammonia packet things under my nose. I'm shivering under a thick wool blanket. My soggy shoes are off, and the cut on my foot is already bandaged up tight. The rain has stopped, and a few rays of sunlight peek through the lingering clouds.

Officer Anderson is in the ambulance with me. He gives me a pat on the shoulder. "You gave me a scare, kid," he says. He shoots me a smile. "You okay?"

"Yeah," I say. I shake my head to get the smell of ammonia out of my nostrils. "I'm alright." I look down at my feet, then at the floor of the ambulance where my shoes lie. The one with the missing sole has been cut into two pieces. "My shoes!" I say, a little too much panic sneaking into my voice.

Anderson chuckles. "Don't worry about those," he says. He motions behind him. A blonde lady in a blue dress stands outside the ambulance. I'm not sure how old she is, but she seems too young to be doing whatever it is that brings her out to a place like this. She smiles and waves when she sees us looking at her.

"That's Rose," he says. "She's a really nice lady. She's going to take care of you and get you everything you need. Including shoes."

"Will you stay with me?" I ask. Anderson looks surprised. To be honest, I kind of surprise myself, too.

"Of course," he says. He rubs his hand over my damp hair. "I'll stay as long as I can."

Officer Anderson drives me to some place downtown. We don't talk much on the way, but we're both fine with that. Rose meets us there and takes us into a room full of beanbag chairs and stuffed animals and old children's books. She leaves the room for a few minutes and comes back with a bundle in her hands. She hands it to me. It's a towel, fresh clothes, and some clean bandages. There's a little bar of soap and a tiny bottle of shampoo on top of the pile.

She shows me into a bathroom and tells me that I can take a shower and get changed if I want to. She leaves, and I start to undress. When I peel off my soggy pants, a crumpled envelope falls to the floor. It's the letter Ms. Odum wanted me to deliver to the school nurse. I know I shouldn't open it, but the curiosity is too much for me to handle.

The words are smudged with the rain, but I can still make them out. *"Please allow Miranda to lie down somewhere quiet. She is not ill, but she is very much in need of rest. Please see to it that no one disturbs her. I will be down after dismissal to see her. If anyone has a problem with this, tell them to come discuss it with me."*

My eyes fill up again. I hug the little note to my chest and take a deep breath before smoothing the wet paper out on the counter to dry. This is definitely a keeper.

I step into the shower and turn the little knob to the hottest setting. The hot water makes me cry, not because it's too hot, but because it's *there*. I can't remember the last time I took an actual hot shower. I've been sort-of cleaning myself with the cold sink water at school for so long that I'd almost forgotten what clean feels like.

I shower until the hot water and soap and shampoo is gone. I bandage my foot and pull on the new clothes--jeans and a pink t-shirt. They're the first new clothes I've had in forever. I look at myself in the mirror. I don't recognize the girl I see. This clean girl in her new clothes is a stranger to me.

I leave the bathroom and return to the beanbag room. When I walk in, Rose and Anderson greet me with big smiles. Rose points to a pair of aqua-blue sneakers on the floor near one of the beanbags.

"Give those a try," she says. "I wasn't sure what size you wear, but I think they'll fit you."

I sit down and pull them on. I burst into tears.

She rushes over to me. "Oh! I'm so sorry!" she says. "Do they hurt you?"

"No," I say through sobs. "They're...they're *perfect*." I cover my face with my now-clean hands and cry some more.

When I'm done with the tears, Rose asks me if it's okay if we talk for a while. I don't know if it's the stress of this whole crazy day or the new clothes or what, but for some reason, I decide that it's finally time to let it all out. For the next few hours, Rose fills several pages of a notebook with the stories I tell her. At several points during the whole process, Rose's eyes fill with tears, and she has to stop writing to wipe them away. A few times, I hear Officer Anderson sniffling and blowing his nose behind me.

But I don't cry this time. I've cried enough. I tell my stories because they need to be told, because they won't be kept secret any longer, because I feel like I'll explode if I don't finally get them out.

Officer Anderson stays until he's called away by some incomprehensible radio chatter. Before he leaves, he wraps me up in a huge hug. "I'll see you around, okay?" he says. His eyes fill with tears again.

"Yeah," I say. "I don't know how I can ever thank you enough. For everything."

"Don't mention it," he says. He nods at Rose and leaves the room.

Rose's cell phone rings. It's someone calling about me. From the half of the conversation I hear, it sounds like they're talking about what they're going to do with me now. I hadn't really thought about it myself, but I guess I can't just stay here. I've been so busy talking about my past that I didn't have a thought for my future.

She ends the call. "That was my boss," she says. "She's found a home for you. Of course with all of this just happening, we don't know how long you'll be there. It's with a lady who just recently signed up for our foster care program. I haven't met her, but the folks around the office say nice things about her."

I nod. Nervousness creeps back in.

We get into her car and drive. It's dark now, and as we leave the city's glow behind, it gets even darker. The farther we drive, the more nervous I become. The thought of staying in a stranger's house for God-knows-how-long is seriously freaking me out. I don't talk, and Rose doesn't try to force me into a conversation. By the time the car turns into the driveway of a little brick house, my heart is pounding.

I can't see very well, but the house looks clean and well-kept. The headlights illuminate a neat row of fall flowers planted in a carefully-tended bed. They cast their bright colors into the night. I look forward to seeing them in the daylight.

The door opens. A person is silhouetted by the light inside. I can't see the face. My heart threatens to explode. I consider turning and running.

Rose takes my hand and walks me closer to the house. I grip her tightly, afraid to let go. She feels my fear.

"It's okay, Miranda," she says.

We walk closer to the open door. I've heard so many horror stories about horrible foster parents. They all play through my mind. I'd give anything right now to be able to run back to the odd comfort of my past misery.

I take a deep breath and step forward. The porch light clicks on. My new guardian's face appears.

My heart leaps.

"Miranda," says Rose. She gestures to the woman waiting to offer me her home and her love. "This is Carol Odum."

She smiles and opens her arms. I run to them.

I look up from her embrace.

Overhead, stars shed their white light through the parting clouds.

Want more?

Check out the free prequel story!

Visit the link below to receive a free eBook and audiobook version!

https://www.jestamper.com/sign-up

Made in United States
North Haven, CT
03 March 2023